but Rachel refused to allow her attraction to Cord to interfere with her plans. Surely she could manage to avoid him for one measly year. She had a big house; Cord would be working, she would be working. They'd hardly run into each other. A year would fly by in a snap.

Rachel heard the shower stop and Cord whistling softly. Suddenly the bathroom door opened, and he stood there in front of her with a little towel around his hips. His hair, shiny and black, was combed back, and water dripped down his neck and chest.

This would be the longest year of her life, she suddenly realized.

Dear Reader,

Welcome to March! Spring is in the air. The birds are chirping, the bees are buzzing...and men and women all over the world are thinking about—love.

Here at Silhouette Desire we take love *very* seriously. We're committed to bringing you six terrific stories all about love each and every month of the year, and this March is no exception.

Let's start with March's *Man of the Month* by Jackie Merritt. It's called *Tennessee Waltz,* and I know you're going to love this story. Next, Naomi Horton returns with *Chastity's Pirate.* (How can you resist a book with a title like this? You just *can't!*) And look for books by Anne Marie Winston, Barbara McCauley, Justine Davis and new-to-Desire Kat Adams.

And in months to come, some of your very favorite authors are coming your way. Look for sensuous romances from the talented pens of Dixie Browning, Lass Small, Cait London, Barbara Boswell...just to name a few.

So go wild with Desire, and start thinking about love.

All the best,

Lucia Macro
Senior Editor

BARBARA McCAULEY

HER KIND OF MAN

SILHOUETTE *Desire*®

Published by Silhouette Books New York

America's Publisher of Contemporary Romance

SILHOUETTE BOOKS
300 East 42nd St., New York, N.Y. 10017

HER KIND OF MAN

ISBN: 0-373-05771-7

First Silhouette Books printing March 1993

Printed in the U.S.A.

Books by Barbara McCauley

Silhouette Desire

Woman Tamer #621
Man From Cougar Pass #698
Her Kind of Man #771

BARBARA McCAULEY

was born and raised in California and has spent a good portion of her life exploring the mountains, beaches and deserts so abundant there. The youngest of five children, she grew up in a small house, and her only chance for a moment alone was to sneak into the backyard with a book and quietly hide away.

With two children of her own now, and a busy household, she still finds herself slipping away to enjoy a good novel. A daydreamer and incurable romantic, she says writing has fulfilled her most incredible dream of all—breathing life into the people in her mind and making them real. She has two loud and demanding Amazon parrots named Fred and Barney, and when she can manage the time, she loves to sink her hands into fresh-turned soil and make things grow.

To Kathy and Janet,
for all your help and inspiration,
to Karen and Patty,
for your support,
and to Russ,
a true horseman who taught me about attitude.

One

She was desperate. Heart-pounding, palm-sweating desperate. If there were any other choice, Rachel Stephens told herself, she'd take it. But time was running out and there was only one solution.

Leaning back against the end stall of the barn, Rachel drew in a shaky breath. She felt as if a stampede were taking place in her stomach. She closed her eyes and slowly counted to ten, forcing herself to relax. The smell of hay and horses reminded her of why she was here, gave her strength not to turn tail and run. In the stall behind her, a bay whinnied and stuck its head over the gate, obviously searching for a treat. Smiling, Rachel brushed the animal's silky nose with her fingertips.

Just outside the barn, only a few feet away, was the possible answer to her problem—Cord Cantrell.

Eyes still closed, she made one last attempt to think of any other solution, something she'd overlooked, *anything*... But there was nothing she hadn't thought of, nothing she hadn't already tried. This move—drastic as it was—was her last hope.

A warm breeze flitted through the open barn, carrying the sounds of the Bar None Ranch to her ears: the hum of a distant tractor, a dog barking, a man's voice—so soft, so gentle, it was barely audible. She kept her eyes closed, straining to hear. The voice was soothing, deep and low. Exactly what she needed right now. Her breathing slowed as she focused, listening to the man.

"Doesn't that feel good?" he whispered. "Here now, darlin', it won't hurt. There's nothing to be afraid of."

The voice reached out and stroked Rachel's shattered nerves, caressed her damp skin.

"That's my sweetheart. I won't hurt you," he soothed.

Absently toying with the end of her blond braid, Rachel tipped her head back and followed the flow of his husky voice as he crooned on. She thought of hot winds and rolling tumbleweeds ... slow dancing and sultry nights ... warm brandy and cool sheets....

Her eyes flew open. *Good heavens!* What was she thinking? She swiped a shaking hand across her brow and noted the perspiration beaded on her temple. Nerves, she told herself, pushing up the sleeves of her pink cotton shirt. That's all it was. Nerves.

She ran through her carefully prepared speech one more time, determined to present herself as calmly and businesslike, as possible. Satisfied she was in control once again, she squared her shoulders and stepped around the corner.

A few yards away, inside a circular pen with a wooden siding, was the man she'd come looking for. His back was to her as he walked a chestnut, holding onto the halter with one hand, while his other hand gently swept a blanket on and off the horse's back.

Rachel knew better than to bother a trainer while he was working with a horse. She stood off to the side, out of the man's view, and watched. The horse, a two-year-old filly, was skittish. It jerked away every time the blanket went on its back, and danced nervously until the blanket was removed. It was a beautiful horse, she thought, a little old perhaps for blanket breaking, but it wasn't uncommon for owners to delay training on a high-spirited animal.

"There you go, baby," came his voice again, soft as a kid glove, "that's a girl." Holding the halter tightly, he swept the blanket on the animal's back and left it. The horse tossed its head and jumped, but the man—his face hidden beneath his Stetson—held a firm grip, sweet-talking as he stroked the filly's glistening neck.

So this was Cord Cantrell, Rachel thought, studying the man. Lean, tall, probably around six foot two or three. Wide, muscled shoulders beneath a blue cotton shirt. Long, well-honed legs wrapped in denim. She watched his work-roughened hand slide over the horse's mane and the sight mesmerized her. A flutter, soft and warm, centered itself low in her stomach.

"Cord!" A shout startled her and she glanced over as a gray-haired man crossed the training arena, kicking dirt with his angry strides. "I told you to get that filly saddle broke by this week and you ain't even got a blanket on her yet."

Frightened, the horse reared at the intrusion and broke away at a run to the far end of the pen. Cord swore under his breath, then slowly, stiffly, he turned to the other man.

"She's been let run too long, Tom," Cord said carefully, each word clipped. "You want a good horse long-term, it takes time."

"Time's something you ain't got," Tom yelled. "That filly ain't worth spit to me like she is. You either get her broke or I give her to Jim at the Rocking J. He knows how to get results fast, and that's all I care about."

At the mention of the other trainer's name, Cord's stance turned rigid. "You take a whip to this filly and you'll break her spirit," he said through gritted teeth. "She won't be good to you or anyone else in a few years."

Tom threw up a hand. "I don't give a damn about a few years. I mean to sell that horse now. I can't be feeding no animal—or man—that don't earn its keep. Just think about that, Cantrell." He turned and stormed off, yelling for a hand to come get the filly and stable her.

Rachel watched Cord's hands slowly clench into fists. His body was taut with controlled rage. As he turned, she saw a muscle flex in his jaw and his eyes narrow. Quietly, deliberately, he walked in her direction.

She ducked back into the barn and pressed her shoulder to the wall, knowing a man's pride wouldn't want a woman witness to an argument where he'd been the clear-cut loser.

He charged into the barn, cursing profusely, his jaw still twitching. He was already three long-legged strides past her when she called to him.

"Mr. Cantrell!"

He stopped short and whirled, as if expecting to face an angry bull. "What!"

One sharp word from him and she lost her voice. She simply stood there, her heart pounding, her mouth half-open. His expression softened slightly the moment he realized he'd just yelled at an innocent bystander.

"Sorry," he muttered, then let out a long breath. "Can I help you?"

It was the first time she'd actually seen his face. His eyes, a deep blue, were still blazing with fury from his confrontation with the other man. His frown, accented by deep creases along the hard set of his mouth, frightened her.

"No, I—I mean yes," she stammered, taking a hesitant step forward. She drew in a slow breath. "Maybe."

He sent her a curious look. "Is this a multiple choice?" he asked.

She cursed the blush she felt working its way up her neck. "What I mean to say is, I hope so."

Cord moved closer. He gave her a quick, cursory scan with his sky-blue eyes. "Well, lady," he drawled, "I certainly hope so, too."

Rachel stiffened. She'd been around enough cowboys to recognize a move, and she'd also been around long enough to know how to block one. "Mr. Cantrell," she said stiffly, raising her chin a notch, "I have a business proposition for you."

He lifted one dark brow. "Oh? And what kind of 'proposition' is that?"

She instantly regretted her choice of words. She regretted being here at all. But there was no turning back now. She felt a bead of perspiration slowly work its way down the middle of her back. Her carefully prepared speech vanished and all she could remember was the bottom line.

"Mr. Cantrell," she said, meeting his gaze, "I want you to marry me."

Cord stared at the woman, thinking perhaps he'd heard wrong. No, he ran her words through his mind again, she'd said it clear as a Montana morning. *I want you to marry me.* It was a joke, of course, and a damn good one, he conceded.

She was an early birthday present, he decided. Russ and Frank had been teasing him that he'd be hitting the ripe old age of thirty-two in a couple of weeks and he'd never married. He looked around the barn, expecting the ranch hands to be hiding in another stall, waiting to jump out and have a good laugh on him, but it appeared the barn was empty. He glanced back at the woman, noted the determined set of her chin, the spark in her gray-green eyes. Damn if she wasn't a pretty little thing.

Well, hell, he thought, tipping his hat back, he liked to think he had a good sense of humor. He'd go along with it.

"Why, sure I'll marry you, honey," he said, moving toward her. He spoke loudly, figuring the boys were hiding somewhere around the corner, or that maybe she had a tape recorder hidden somewhere on her. He couldn't imagine where, though. Her jeans stretched tightly over her long, slender legs, and her blouse, open at the neck, revealed smooth, white skin.

This joke was getting better all the time.

Eyes wide, she retreated from him until he'd backed her against a stall. He placed a hand on either side of her and leaned close. She smelled like a spring meadow and tall, cool grass; the heat of her body touched him and he suddenly thought of soft, damp skin and her long legs wrapped around him. His body instantly responded to that image.

"In fact—" he glanced over her shoulder into the stall behind her "—we could start the honeymoon right now." He lowered his mouth two inches away from hers and whispered, "Ever make love on soft, fresh hay, darlin'?"

Shocked, Rachel didn't move. She *couldn't* move. If she did, her breasts would brush against Cord's chest. She knew instinctively that that would be a big mistake. He hadn't actually touched her, but she felt as if he'd consumed her, pulled her in and turned her inside out. Her knees were the consistency of warm taffy; her pulse thudded in her temples. There was the briefest, most disturbing sensation of lying on her back, hay scratching her bare skin.

The image shocked her and brought her back to reality. She wasn't completely sure where she'd lost control, or if she'd ever even had it, but this situation was definitely out of hand.

"Mr. Cantrell," she said, placing her palms on his rock-hard chest. She pushed. He stayed put. "Mr. Cantrell," she repeated with more determination, then said softly, urgently, "Please."

He went still; a look of bewilderment darkened his blue eyes. And something else: desire. She felt a twinge of apprehension—or perhaps anticipation? He straightened, then slowly moved away from her. She dropped her hands from his chest and shoved them into the front pocket of her jeans.

"I—I'm sorry," she said, stepping away from him. "I should have explained first. I...just got so nervous."

Cord regarded her suspiciously. "Russ didn't put you up to this?"

"Russ?" She shook her head. "I don't know Russ. Nobody put me up to this."

"This isn't about my birthday?" He looked disappointed. "You're not going to break into song, or do a striptease?"

"What? No!" she gasped. "I'm not a singing telegram, and no one hired me. I meant what I said. I want you to marry me."

He simply stared at her, obviously too stunned to comment.

"Please," she said, meeting his gaze, "just hear me out."

He leaned back against the stall, folding his arms casually. "I'm all ears."

And all man, the thought came to her unbidden. She booted it right out of her mind, then drew in a breath to steady herself.

"I realize, of course, how ridiculous this may sound to you," she said, raking a hand through her long bangs. "But if I don't find a husband—soon—I'll be forced to sell my ranch."

Cord's expression was skeptical. "I never heard of any law in Texas that says a woman has to be married to own a ranch."

He still didn't believe her, she realized. Anger at him, at herself, at the entire situation, sliced through her. She narrowed her eyes and fixed him with a cool look. "I'm dead serious about this, Mr. Cantrell." The determination she heard in her own voice surprised her. "And I assure you I'll make it worth your while."

Cord looked at the beautiful young woman in front of him. Her cheeks were flushed, her eyes bright with determination, her mouth wide and inviting. "Lady," he said, sweeping his eyes over her long, lithe body, "there's no doubt in my mind being married to you would be worth my while."

Her eyes lighted with anger. "I'm not part of the deal, Mr. Cantrell," she said coldly. "I only want the marriage to regain control of my ranch, then after a year, a quiet divorce and we go our separate ways. What you would gain is a place to work for the next year without a jackass of an owner telling you how to break a horse."

His jaw flexed as he realized she'd witnessed the argument with Tom. It had taken every ounce of willpower not to lay the man out flat.

"And," she continued with what he thought was a note of satisfaction, "I will grant you the deed to one thousand acres of land in Abilene my husband left to me in my trust. I have no use for it, but if you're interested, you could set up a ranch of your own. If not, you could always sell it."

One thousand acres? He felt as if he'd just been kicked in the gut. *If he was interested?* There wasn't a horse trainer alive that didn't dream of owning his own ranch, being his own boss. The lady definitely had his attention.

"What do you mean," he asked, " 'regain control' of your ranch?"

The bay snorted loudly, as if emphasizing Cord's question. Rachel turned to the horse and reached out to stroke its neck. "Two years ago," she began, keeping her eyes on the horse, "my husband, Michael, died in a plane crash. There was a stipulation in his will that all the financial and administrative dealings of his estate, including the ranch, would be left in charge of his brother, Earl, until I remarried."

Cord raised both brows. "Why would he do that?"

Rachel looked sharply at him. "That's really no business of yours."

Cord pushed away from the stall he'd been leaning on. "You just asked me to marry you, and you're telling me it's none of my business why?" He gave a sarcastic laugh. "How 'bout you grab that shovel behind you and I direct you to the cow pen? If you're going to be shoveling something, it might as well be the real thing."

Rachel watched as Cord touched the tip of his hat. "It's been a pleasure, ma'am," he said to her, then turned on his heels to leave.

"Wait." He paused when she called out to him, then turned to face her, hands on his hips. He was right, Rachel conceded. He did have a right to ask. It was just so... humiliating to explain.

She sighed deeply, closing her eyes for a moment while she gathered her words. "Michael," she began, opening her eyes again, "was a man who liked to make decisions. Not only for himself, but for everyone around him." She smiled wryly. "Especially me. He... meant well, of course," she went on hesitantly. "But it never occurred to him that I was capable of making decisions for myself. He always felt he had to protect me, take care of me. He never would have dreamed that I would even consider running the Circle T myself."

"The Circle T?" Cord straightened. Everyone had heard of the Circle T. It was about a hundred and fifty miles due west of here, close to Sweetwater. He remembered talk of the owner's death a ways back, but had forgotten the name. Until now. Stephens. Michael Stephens.

"I've heard of your husband," Cord said. "If my memory serves me, he was an oil tycoon and businessman who reportedly bought the Circle T as a birthday present for his wife."

Rachel shook her head. "That was the story he told the papers, but actually, the ranch was one of the assets of a large company he purchased. His intention had always been to sell the Circle T when he found the right buyer at the right price."

She moved away from Cord and stood at the open door of the barn. The April breeze was warm, but felt good against her hot skin. It was only ten-thirty and already the day promised to be a scorcher. Someone else was working a horse in the pen now and in the distance, a ranch hand was bathing a sorrel mare while a white-and-black dog ran around the horse, barking furiously. She turned back to Cord.

"All my life I've lived in one big, cold house or condominium after another. Wherever my father's continual scramble for corporate success took him, that's where we went. I hadn't realized before I married Michael it would be the same way for us. In the two years we were married, I lived in four different states and five different houses." She looked back out at the corral. "The first time I set foot on Circle T land, about six months before Michael's death, I fell in love with the place. The minute I walked in the house, I felt the life there, the pulse. I felt like I'd come home."

She folded her arms and looked at Cord. "I asked my husband if we could live there, but he said it wasn't convenient for him. He had a business in Fort Worth at the time and he'd already leased a home in Dallas for us. I had to settle for an occasional weekend when Michael would fly down to check out his 'investment.'"

A slow smile spread across Rachel's mouth. "Earl was aghast when I moved onto the Circle T after Michael's death. I believe his term for ranch life is *uncivilized*. He insisted I put the property up for sale, but I refused. Since he can't sell without my signature, it's been a constant battle between us."

"Ranching's not an easy thing for a woman," Cord said knowingly. Rachel laughed and the sound flitted through him, charming him, making him smile, as well.

"Especially not a spoiled city gal, right?" At his nod, she added, "Believe me, cowboy, I've heard it enough times to almost believe it. Thing is, I heard it so many times, I sort of got stubborn about it. For once in my life I determined that I was going to take a stand."

At last, Cord felt he was beginning to understand. He watched her toss her blond braid defiantly over her shoulder.

"You mean to tell me," he said slowly, "that you'd actually get married to a man you don't even know just to get rid of your brother-in-law?"

Her face turned bright red, but she straightened and met his gaze. "Earl has been running the ranch into the ground for the last two years. He buys inferior hay, pays the hands late and refuses to repair anything that breaks. On top of that, the man is an arrogant ass. My trainer quit last week after Earl informed him he'd have to take a cut in pay. Without a trainer, what few clients I have left will soon be gone, too."

Cord knew that no horse ranch could survive for long without a trainer. He couldn't help but wonder if that had been her brother-in-law's intention. Without even meeting the man, he instantly disliked him.

Rachel bent down and scooped up a handful of hay. "The Circle T has given my life a meaning I've never experienced before," she said, letting the hay sift through her fingers. "For the first time, I feel a responsibility, a need to work at something. There's no way for me to make you truly understand my feelings toward the Circle T, Mr. Cantrell, but I can say it's the one thing in my life, perhaps the first thing, that's made me understand commitment."

There was something in Rachel's eyes, something in the tone of her voice, that made Cord believe her. Still, it was difficult for him to understand why a woman as beautiful as she was would choose such a hard life.

"What about your family?" Cord asked. "Why don't you go to them for help?"

Her eyes turned icy at his question. "My father says when I'm ready to come to my senses and sell the ranch, he'll be more than happy to have me come live with my mother and him in Germany. Until then, I'm on my own." She scooped up another handful of hay and tossed it. "What he doesn't understand is that's the way I want it—to be on my own."

Cord shook his head. He still couldn't figure this woman out. "If you don't mind my saying so," he said, "you don't exactly look like a woman I'd accidentally put a feed bag on. I would think you'd have a hundred stallions fighting over you. Why would you come to me, a stranger, and make this offer?"

She brushed her hands off on her jeans and straightened. "I may be desperate, but I'm practical, as well. I hired a private investigator to get me a list of the single trainers that would meet the criteria I set. Your name was at the top of that list." She let out a long, weary breath. "Short of poison, and believe me, I've considered it, marriage is the only thing left to me."

From the tone of her voice, Cord thought her statement sounded more like a prison term than a joyous union. But then, hadn't that always been the way he viewed marriage?

The way his mother had viewed marriage...

He thought hard about what this woman proposed to him. A year to be his own boss, no one telling him what to do. Training horses the way he wanted. And then, after a year...

The chance to have his own ranch, if not for now, then for the future.

No. He gave himself a mental shake. Even if it was only for a year, marriage was still marriage. He looked at Rachel, felt his body tighten as he drank in the sight of her. He was thirsty for a woman. He hadn't been with one for a long time. But, tempted as he was, he wasn't about to think with anything other than his brain. Still, if the lady had included herself in the deal...

"Mrs. Stephens," he said, removing his hat and raking a hand through his dark hair, "I'm sure that later I'll call myself a fool ten times over, but I'm just not the marrying type. I appreciate your 'proposition'—" he smiled "—but I'm afraid I have to turn you down."

She stood there, rigid, her cheeks flushed, her shoulders squared, and met his gaze. "I understand completely, Mr. Cantrell," she said stiffly, but not in anger. "Thank you for your time."

She reached into her back pocket and pulled out a business card. "If you decide you might like to discuss this further, I'm staying here until I...conclude my business."

She meant until she found a husband. As Cord watched her turn and walk away, it suddenly dawned on him that she'd be going to the next ranch. Making the same "proposition" to the next cowboy. For some strange reason he didn't like that one little bit. He felt as if a fist had grabbed hold of his insides. He ran out of the barn.

"Mrs. Stephens!"

She was stepping into a black pickup when she turned.

"What's your name—your first name?"

"Rachel," she answered, then closed the door and started the truck. As she drove off, she stuck her head out of the window and smiled widely at him, as if to let him know she held no grudges. Business was business, after all.

But there was something in her eyes, in the smile itself, that he couldn't quite put his finger on, and even as he walked back to the barn, that smile still lingered.

Two

The waiting was driving Rachel insane. She'd neatly bitten one fingernail down to a nub and almost worn a path in the motel room's carpeting waiting for a return call from the trainer at the Rocking M. He was the second name on her list, a man named Luke Harding. After her "meeting" with Cord, Rachel had decided it best not to show up unannounced.

She thought back on the morning and a fierce wave of embarrassment washed over her again. She couldn't even remember how she managed to walk away so calmly, considering the way her knees had been shaking. The expression on Cord's face when she'd asked him to marry her was still etched in her mind. He'd looked at her as if she were a crazy woman.

With a loud groan, Rachel sank down on the bed. Why wouldn't he think she was a mental case? *She* certainly did. And here she was, waiting for a phone call from another man so she could put herself through this stupidity, and most probably rejection, all over again.

She pushed her hair back from her face and sighed. What had Earl made her sink to? Gallivanting around the country begging cowboys to marry her? She lay on the bed and closed her eyes, listening to the rattle of the air conditioner. How could she have ever thought this insane scheme would work?

And how could she have known that the first man she proposed to would sweep her off her feet like a Texas twister?

Had he noticed? She'd practically melted when he'd pressed her against the stall and whispered in her ear. She could still smell him: leather, horses and his own masculine scent. Her insides had felt like molten lava, her heart had hammered so loudly, he must have heard it. Of course he noticed, she thought with despair. A man like Cord Cantrell knew exactly what he did to a woman. She wouldn't doubt that he had women proposing to him all the time. To him, this was probably a regular occurrence.

She was glad he'd turned her down. He was all wrong for her. Two years of living under Michael Stephens's thumb had taught her a lot about men. At twenty-two, fresh out of college, Rachel had been impressed with Michael's sophistication and position. His charm and attention had bowled her over, and she'd fallen in love with him immediately, marrying him after a whirlwind romance.

From the first day of that marriage, however, she realized that power and money were the priorities in his life. And control. It was Michael's decision, or no decision. Rachel doubted that he'd ever considered the possibility that she even *had* an opinion of her own, that just maybe she hadn't wanted to live in a town house in Palm Beach, or a condominium in Dallas. Her parents had taught her to be the obedient daughter. For Michael she'd been the obedient wife. He'd kept her in her place like a bug on its back and she'd never once had the courage to disagree with him.

But she wasn't that woman anymore. Michael's unexpected death had devastated her, but it had made her grow up, as well. Her sudden independence terrified her at first, then slowly, as she learned to make decisions and choices for herself, she reveled in her newfound freedom. If she ever married again—really married—she would choose a man who could love her for what she was, not for what he wanted, or expected, her to be.

Cord Cantrell, though obviously very different from Michael, still had the same traits. Rachel recognized the power in Cord to control and mold to his will not only animals, but people, too. Especially women. She was lucky he hadn't wanted to marry her. What a mistake that would have been.

The phone rang and she bolted upright. It had to be Luke Harding. She started to grab for the phone, then pulled back. Could she really go through this humiliation again? She shook her head. The phone rang two more times. She bit her knuckle.

What if it were Cord? She'd given him her number. It wouldn't hurt to just talk to him, would it?

She picked up the phone on the fifth ring. "Hello?" Her voice cracked. She cleared her throat. "Hello."

"Ms. Stephens?"

It wasn't Cord. She detested the feeling of disappointment that swam though her. "Yes."

"This is Luke Harding, from the Rocking M. I got a message you called, ma'am?"

She simply sat there, the receiver in her hand. She couldn't do this again. She couldn't.

"Ma'am? You still there?"

She had to. She had nothing else to lose, everything to gain. "Yes, yes, I'm still here." She felt as if a hand were clenched around her throat. "I...wonder if you...could meet with me, Mr. Harding. It's a little complicated to talk about over the phone, but I have—" she avoided the word *proposition* "—an important matter I'd like to discuss with you."

"Why, sure, ma'am," he said, his drawl thickening, "I'd be happy to come on over."

Rachel glanced around her hotel room. Not exactly the best place to meet a cowboy. Outside the window, the restaurant sign across the street caught her eye. "How about The Red Eye Bar and Grill, the one across from Mave's Motel. Say around six?" It was already five. That would give her an hour to get ready. Sixty minutes.

"Six at The Red Eye," he repeated.

"I'll leave my name at the front so you can find me," she said, then hung up the phone. Her stomach felt like a pretzel. She laid back on the bed, letting out a long, shaky moan. Twice in one day she was going to make a fool out of herself. Twice. She covered her face with her hands.

Would Mr. Harding be as good-looking as Cord? she wondered. In her mind, she saw those deep blue eyes boring into hers, his breath hot on her neck as he asked her if she'd ever made love in fresh hay. The memory alone sent shivers running up her spine.

Damn! She sat up abruptly. She had to stop thinking about Cord Cantrell. He'd turned her down and that was that. Thank God. How would she have possibly gotten through one entire year and stayed out of the man's bed, when in a mere ten minutes he had her wondering what it would be like to make love in a pile of hay?

Yessiree, she decided, rising from the bed and heading for the shower. She was pretty lucky, after all.

Six hours after Rachel Stephens drove off the Bar None Ranch, Cord finally figured out what he'd seen in the beautiful blonde's eyes.

Disappointment.

As if frozen by the thought, he stopped midstride and stood in front of his tiny house, too stunned to move. *Disappointment?* Nah, he shook his head and gave a chuckle. Why would the woman be disappointed? She had a list of other men, men just as qualified—more, probably—than he was, if her private investigator had done his job well. Cord stomped up his front steps, kicking the dust off his boots.

What if the P.I. hadn't done his job well? Cord wondered. Frowning, he opened the door and stepped inside the living room. What if the man had overlooked some seedy secret and one of those guys— maybe the guy Rachel married—was some kind of a weirdo? What would she do then, after she'd already hooked up with him?

What the lady does is no concern of yours, Cantrell.

Cord unbuttoned his damp, dusty shirt and headed for the refrigerator. A cold beer would dissolve these unsettling thoughts, he decided, pulling a can off the bottom shelf. Rachel looked more than capable of handling herself. Hell, that lady had more ba—he stopped and popped the lid—bravado, than half the men he knew.

He eased himself down on a leather armchair and took a long pull on his beer. Closing his eyes, he saw hair the color of sun-ripened wheat, soft, feminine curves that made his hands itch and bright green eyes filled first with desperation, then embarrassment, and finally...disappointment.

There was that word again. Cord held the cool can to his sweaty forehead. Why would she be disappointed? A woman who looked like Rachel wouldn't have a problem finding a man to marry her. She'd have her pick. Just because Cord Cantrell was too stupid to know what was good for him, didn't mean the other men on that damn list would be. He looked at the clock over his stove. It was just after five. She'd had all day to find the next trainer and make the same offer. He didn't doubt she was strolling happily down the aisle right now.

He rose and walked to his front window, pushing back the faded brown curtains as he stared out at the training ring. His boss was working a horse and from the sound of his hollering, the horse was being less than cooperative. Cord flinched at the sound of a whip on the animal's flesh. His gut twisted and it was all he could do not to walk out there and turn that whip on the bastard himself. Give him a taste of his own medicine. The beer turned sour in Cord's mouth and he slammed it down on a table, swearing hotly.

He swung away from the window, unbuckling his belt as he moved toward the bedroom where he pulled off his boots, then his jeans, and tossed them in a pile with his socks and shirt.

As he started to turn he noticed a white business card on the floor beside his jeans. He picked it up and turned it over. *Mave's Motel.* Rachel had written in her name and room number beneath the motel's address. He stared at it for a long moment before he flipped it back onto the pile of dirty clothes and headed for the shower.

The Red Eye Bar and Grill offered little in the way of decor and menu, but much in local color and flavor. Based on the crowd already assembled around the bar, it was a popular hangout not only for townspeople, but ranch hands and cowboys, as well. Fascinated, Rachel glanced around the room. Smoke filled the air, sawdust covered the floor and a sweet country song poured out of a jukebox in the corner. The smell of barbecue sauce and grilled chicken made Rachel's uneasy stomach rumble.

The place was a far cry from the elegant dining Michael had always insisted on, but for some reason, Rachel felt more comfortable here than in a stuffy French restaurant. She gave her name at the front desk, then followed a redheaded hostess to a corner booth.

Rachel sat, then crossed her legs as she looked around the room, carefully avoiding any eye contact with the men she knew had watched her walk in and sit down. She was fresh meat in a lion's den here, she realized, and hoped that Mr. Harding arrived before she got pounced on.

Still, nervous as the stares made her, Rachel couldn't help but feel a sense of satisfaction. She hated to admit it, but her ego was still smarting from Cord's rejection this morning and she'd felt a certain feminine need to look her best tonight. She'd washed her hair and let it dry naturally in loose curls that fell just below her shoulders. Her makeup—though soft—had been applied with excruciating care. She'd even gone into town and bought a new dress, though now that she had it on she wished she hadn't let the salesgirl talk her into it. The dress, a white cotton knit with long sleeves and a V-neck, hugged her body like a second skin.

Rachel realized now, though, that it hadn't actually been the salesgirl who had convinced her. It had been her own rebellious nature. When it had occurred to her that it was a dress Michael would never have approved of, the decision to buy it had been made. That and a casual comment by the salesgirl guaranteeing Rachel it was a dress that would get a woman her man every time.

She suddenly realized she was about to find out if that guarantee was good.

The hostess was pointing at her, directing a man in her direction. Rachel thought briefly of running as he made his way across the room, but the corner left her no way out.

She was stuck.

"Ms. Stephens?"

She didn't want to do this anymore. It didn't matter that he was good-looking and had a nice smile. She just simply couldn't do this. "Yes." She extended her hand and he took it. No tingles. No change in pulse rate. Nothing.

Relief poured over her.

"Rachel, please," she said, smiling, then gestured to the seat across from her. "Won't you sit down?" She'd buy him dinner, explain to him that she'd made a mistake, then thank him for his time.

"Mr. Harding," she began, "I realize how crazy this is going to sound, but—"

"Hi, Rachel, honey." She turned at the sound of the deep, familiar voice.

Cord!

"Sorry I'm late," he said, slipping next to her on the bench. "I had a little problem at the ranch and had to straighten it out."

Sorry I'm late? She stared at him in disbelief. What in the world was he talking about, and what was he doing here? She started to ask him just that as she recalled his greeting.

Rachel *honey?*

"*Mr.* Cantrell—"

"Shoot, you don't have to introduce Luke to me," Cord said, sticking his hand out to the other man. "How's life at the Rocking M?"

She groaned silently, clenching her back teeth while somehow managing a smile. It shouldn't have surprised her that Cord knew Luke Harding. Most trainers knew, or had at least heard of, each other. She'd just never expected to be sitting with *two* of the men on her list. At least, not at the same time.

Luke gave Cord a questioning smile and took his hand. "Can't complain. How's the Bar None?"

"Looking for a trainer, last I heard." Cord waved the waitress down and signaled for drinks. "I quit this afternoon."

Quit? Rachel stared at Cord's profile, too stunned to speak. She'd barely gotten over the initial shock of seeing him here, and now he'd thrown her another curve. Why had he quit? Unless . . . No, she dismissed the thought. He couldn't have quit because of her. He'd turned her offer down flat.

So what was he doing here? And why was she so happy to see him, dammit?

Hoping a drink would settle her frayed nerves, Rachel ordered a glass of white wine. She sat stiffly beside Cord, careful not to brush up against him, and listened to the men reminisce. From their conversation, she surmised they'd worked on a ranch together somewhere in Wyoming.

Maybe she should call the rest of the men on her list and invite them over, too, she thought dismally. Just get this business over in one fell swoop. Surely at least one man out of the bunch would be interested. Unlike Mr. Cord Cantrell, she fumed, resting one elbow on the table and cupping her chin in her palm.

He'd hardly given her a second look since he'd walked in. It annoyed her all the more because she was having a hard time keeping her eyes off him. Every detail seemed to fascinate her: his white, long-sleeved shirt against his tanned skin, a scar that crossed the knuckles on his right hand, the lines beside his mouth that deepened every time he smiled.

The waitress set their drinks down, gaining an appreciative smile from Cord. Maybe she should send this dress back, after all, Rachel decided, tugging at the hem. Just the smell of him—a mixture of soap and shaving cream and pure, unadulterated male—had her on edge. His thigh brushed hers and, even with their clothes on, his touch burned into her skin, then raced through her blood. She felt as if she'd been branded.

She couldn't breathe with him sitting so close to her, but the wall prevented her from moving away.

She'd lost control here before she'd even started, she realized with exasperation. Determined to right the situation, and forget about Cord, she flashed a smile at Luke.

Cord watched Rachel's blatant attempt at flirtation with Luke and was filled with a curious mixture of amusement and jealousy. While it was obvious that Rachel was not an experienced tease, that dress she was wearing, and the way her hair looked as if she'd just tumbled out of bed, would have any man snapping to attention. Lord knew it was all he could do not to drag the woman off and show her just how strongly she'd attracted *his* attention. And based on the way Luke's eyes had darkened at her smile, Cord was going to have to intervene quickly.

"So, Luke," Cord said loudly, forcing the other man to look at him, "rumor has it that gelding you bought last year is going to take the prize at Fort Worth this year."

"He stands a chance," Luke answered modestly, but the pride in his eyes was unmistakable. As Luke went on about the horse, Cord felt himself relax and settled back in the booth, pleased with himself at the diversion. Rachel, on the other hand, stiffened beside him and he noticed the slight narrowing of her eyes as she glanced sharply at him.

"Excuse me," Rachel said. Luke and Cord both looked at her. "I'm sorry to interrupt, but, Cord, I wonder if you'd mind if I had a moment to speak with Mr. Harding, *alone?*" Holding Cord's gaze, she emphasized the last word.

Luke shifted uncomfortably, then looked at Cord, as if asking for permission. Trainers were blatantly territorial—with their ranches and their women—and though Rachel hadn't realized it, Cord had already made it clear to Luke that Rachel was out of bounds. The look that Cord gave Luke now, though subtle, was distinctly understood by the other man.

"I'm sorry, Mrs. Stephens," Luke said, rising, "but I'm afraid I'll have to call you later. I just stopped by to tell you I'd forgotten I had another appointment tonight." He rose from the table. "Sorry if I put you out any."

"By the way," Cord said, slipping an arm around Rachel, "did Rachel get a chance to tell you we're getting married?"

Her mouth dropped open. She watched in stunned amazement as Luke shook Cord's hand in congratulations, then tipped his hat to her.

This was too much, Rachel thought, but because she didn't want to cause a scene, she sat there, waiting until Luke had left before she twisted out of Cord's firm grip and faced him. "What exactly was that all about?"

"What?" He took a casual sip of his beer.

"You know what, *honey*," she drawled sarcastically, imitating him. "I was in the middle of a . . . business meeting and you interrupted. I want to know why you came here, and I especially want to know why you told Mr. Harding that you and I are getting married. You seem to forget you turned me down," Rachel reminded him. "Mr. Harding—"

"Is not right for you," Cord finished for her, folding his arms.

"Not right for me?" Her voice cracked. It was on the tip of her tongue to tell him she'd changed her mind anyway, that she had no intention of asking Luke Harding to marry her, but the arrogant look on Cord's face stopped her. "He looks perfectly 'right' to me," she said defiantly. "And what business is it of yours, anyway?"

"I'm making it my business," he stated flatly. "And I'm telling you, it won't work with Luke."

"What are you," Rachel snapped, "the local Cupid? I'm not looking for love, Mr. Cantrell, just a husband, a partner, if you will. One year, that's all. When it's time to pick a real husband, I'll worry about what's right or not. For now, Luke Harding looked just fine to me."

There was an imperceptible narrowing of Cord's eyes, but Rachel paid no attention to it. "Thank you very much, Mr. Cantrell," she went on. "You just managed to chase away what I considered to be a strong business opportunity."

He laughed. "Business opportunity? Is that what you call getting married these days?"

The sound of Cord's laugh rolled through her like a warm wind. "In this case, yes." She moved away from him. "And the way my list is dwindling, I may have to place an ad with an employment agency."

"Who else is on that list?" Cord asked suddenly.

"That's none of your business."

"Rachel," he said impatiently, "there isn't a trainer within two hundred miles of here I haven't met. I know things your private investigator couldn't possibly have found out."

Rachel hesitated. That's why she'd hired an investigator, of course, to make sure none of the men had past histories that might prove dangerous or inconvenient. But what if something about one of these men had been missed? Something important. Reluctantly, she reached into her purse and pulled out the list.

"Well," she said, clearing her throat, "there's Pete Wilkes over at—"

"Jensen's Ranch," Cord finished. "Pete's all right, if you don't mind he's got four kids in three different states."

Rachel swallowed. Her information didn't include that. "And then there's Wes Smith at the W Oak—"

"The first guy you'd invite to a party," Cord interjected, smiling. "He knows every lady from here to Abilene."

Rachel's lips tightened. "Jim Atwood at the—"

Swearing, Cord ripped the list out of Rachel's hand. She gasped when he grabbed hold of her shoulders. "Men like Atwood use a whip for pleasure," Cord said through clenched teeth. His eyes were narrowed, angry. "Horse or woman, it doesn't matter to him." He gave her a shake then released her. "What the hell kind of investigator did you hire, anyway? Senile or blind?"

His outburst frightened her. He'd made her feel like a child. A foolish, silly child. Rubbing her arms, she straightened her shoulders and lifted her chin. "You were on that list, also, Cord. What should I know about you?"

His gaze burned into her. "Every man has a dark side, Rachel. I'm no different. You want to save your ranch. I can help you do that. You'll have to trust me when I tell you I won't hurt you or embarrass you."

Something told her that Cord Cantrell was probably the worst choice for a husband she could make. He scared her, but it had nothing to do with violence or debauchery. What it had to do with was the way her pulse sped up whenever he looked at her and the electricity that shot through her when he touched her. She had no idea how to handle those feelings when it came to a man like Cord.

"Why," she asked him quietly, "did you change your mind?"

He smiled. "It's not every day a beautiful lady proposes, Rachel. Once I got my wits about me, I hightailed it over here. You weren't in your room, but your truck was parked out front, so I figured you were around somewhere."

She nodded and took a sip of her wine. "Tell me, Cord. What's wrong with Mr. Harding?"

Cord grinned. "Lack of determination."

She couldn't help but laugh. "Something you have?"

"You can bet on it."

"If you marry me," Rachel said, "that's exactly what I'll be doing."

He looked down at her. "So the offer still stands?"

She met his steady gaze and nodded. "The offer still stands, cowboy."

He raised his glass and touched it to hers. "So what are we waiting for?"

Three

———

"**B**y the power vested in me, I now pronounce you husband and wife."

Cord stared at Judge Wooder, then swallowed hard. *Married.* Stunned by the realization, he glanced down at Rachel's hand clasped in his. Her fingers were buried in his palm like slivers of ice and the slender gold band she now wore marked her as his wife.

Wife.

One of the witnesses, a grandmotherly clerk, gave Cord a syrupy smile, while the second witness, a fence-post thin brunette, looked on with an expression resembling a sick calf.

The walls inside the judge's chamber were suddenly closing in on him.

"Are you going to kiss the bride?" The judge peered at Cord over thick, heavy-rimmed glasses.

Kiss the bride? Damn if he didn't feel like a kid on his first date. Cord looked at Rachel, who was staring stiffly at his chest. Even in heels, the top of her head just barely came to his chin. The off-white conservative suit she wore was formal, tailored for the look of self-confidence, success. A good choice, he reasoned. This was, after all, a business meeting. A merger, so to speak. Even he had dusted off and aired out his one suit for today. So why then, if this was strictly business, did he find himself wondering if under Rachel's prim-and-proper exterior there was lace and silk and soft, heated skin?

Rachel focused on the tiny gray polka dots on Cord's tie. Her insides were tied up in knots and his hesitation to kiss her twisted her frazzled nerves even more. In the three days' waiting period after they'd applied for a marriage license—which Cord had insisted on paying for—she'd alternately spent her time wondering how to tell him she'd changed her mind, and worrying that he had changed his. When he'd showed up outside the courthouse this morning, on time, she'd actually been surprised. But not nearly as surprised as when he slipped the ring on her finger a few moments ago. His thoughtfulness had tugged at her heart, and also embarrassed her because she hadn't bought him one.

The charcoal pin-striped suit he wore had surprised her also. Except for the boots and Stetson, he looked like every other high-powered executive she'd ever met, not like a cowboy who made his living by hard, physical work. As handsome as he looked, she decided she liked him better in denim.

The judge cleared his throat. "I said, you may kiss the bride now."

"Oh . . . ah, right," Cord mumbled, then turned to her.

He took her by the arms and pulled her close. Her heart slammed in her chest, her insides jumped.

Oh, God, not now! She grabbed at her stomach. The sudden look of terror in Rachel's green eyes stopped Cord. Her cheeks turned white, her eyes grew wide. Surprised, he watched as she whirled around to face the judge.

"Do you have a bathroom here?" she asked quickly.

Startled by her question, the man simply pointed to a door behind him. Rachel clapped a hand over her mouth and darted from the room.

All eyes stared at the closed bathroom door. The judge raised his eyebrows and turned to Cord, silently questioning him.

"She gets like this in the morning," Cord said, shaking his head sympathetically. "Doctor said it will pass in a month or two."

Before the judge could respond, Rachel stepped out of the bathroom. Her face was bright red. "Excuse me," she mumbled, then quickly gathered her purse.

"Let's get you some air, sweetheart." Cord took her by the arm. He smiled at the witnesses, who were both staring at him with wide eyes. "Judge—" he extended his hand "—we're much obliged to you for fitting us in so quickly."

The judge nodded and took Cord's hand, offering his congratulations. "Hope you feel better soon," he said to Rachel. "My wife had the same thing with our third boy. Poor thing couldn't keep a bite down for months."

Rachel gasped, but Cord shuffled her from the room before she could speak. Outside the judge's chamber, she jerked her arm out of Cord's hand and faced him.

"Just what exactly did you tell him?" Her eyes narrowed.

"Exactly?" Cord shrugged. "Nothing."

She folded her arms and lifted her chin. "How come I don't believe you?"

He smiled. "Now is that any way to start a marriage, Mrs. Cantrell, by doubting my word?"

Mrs. Cantrell. Rachel stared at Cord's face, his words striking her full force. She'd been so busy worrying over a hundred other things—such as marrying a complete stranger—she'd forgotten the small detail of a name change. She was now Rachel *Cantrell.* Mrs. Cord Cantrell. The room started to spin and before she could protest, Cord wrapped an arm around her and guided her to a chair in the lobby.

"What's going on with you, Rachel?" His eyes grew dark. "You aren't, are you?"

"What?"

"Pregnant."

"No!" She brought a hand to her face and noticed how cold her cheek was. Impending motherhood was definitely not something she need be concerned about. She frowned at Cord. "Of course not."

"So then what was that all about in there?" He nodded back to the judge's chamber. "It's not exactly the highest compliment to the groom when the bride loses her cookies after the ceremony."

She felt the heat of a blush creep up her neck. "I— I'm sorry...sometimes when I get...nervous," she said, drawing in a sharp breath, "I get a queasy stomach."

His gaze was thoughtful as he watched her for a moment. "When was the last time you ate?"

She had to stop and think. "Ah, I had some coffee this morning and—"

"That's what I thought." He shook his head. "And how much sleep have you had while we were waiting out the time period on the marriage license?"

Sleep? She tried to remember. Just snatches here and there. "Cord, I really don't see what—"

"Come on." He pulled her up, practically carrying her. "There's a coffee shop next door, I'm going to feed you, then I'm getting you in bed."

Bed! She dug her feet into the carpeting and stopped cold. "We had an agreement, Cord—" she tried to twist away from him, but he tightened his hold "—and just because I'm too tired to think straight doesn't mean you can change things now."

Exasperation etched the deep lines beside Cord's mouth. Rachel suddenly realized he was just as tired as she was.

"Ah, ye of so little faith," he said, sighing. He pulled her snugly against him and tilted her chin up with his index finger. He gazed down into her eyes with a mixed expression of disappointment and annoyance.

"Rachel, honey," he said, lowering his voice, "when, and if, we get between the sheets together, you can bet it won't be when we're both too tired to do anything about it." A shiver ran through her as he traced the line of her jaw. "And you can also bet I won't be dragging you there kicking and screaming."

His statement, issued with such complete certainty, left her speechless. And even as he ushered her through the glass doors of the courthouse to a restaurant next door, she was wondering what she had gotten herself into.

It was dark when she finally woke. Disoriented, Rachel blinked several times, trying to remember where she was. She closed her eyes again as it all came flooding back to her: the wedding, an awkward lunch with Cord, his gentle concern when he brought her back to the hotel and insisted she climb into bed. His tone had been more fatherly than husbandly and for that she was appreciative. As exhausted as she was, she doubted she could have resisted those blue eyes and beguiling smile.

But why was it so dark? she wondered, sitting up in bed. Cord must have drawn the heavy plastic drapes that shut out the light. She fumbled for the clock on the bed stand and turned it toward her.

Eight o'clock!

She'd been sleeping for seven hours!

With a moan, Rachel dragged her fingers through her tangled hair and swung her legs around to sit on the edge of the bed. She knew the stress of waiting those three days, not to mention the actual wedding, had taken its toll on her, but this was ridiculous. She never slept in the middle of the day. She'd intended to rest for about an hour, then pack her things and be ready when Cord returned from the Bar None with his horses. It was about a three-hour drive to Sweetwater and they could have easily made it before dark. Why hadn't he woke her up?

The sudden thought that maybe he hadn't come back sent a cold chill up her spine. She picked up her pillow and hugged it to her, waiting a moment before she rose and moved to the window, pulling back the drapes as she looked out into the parking lot.

His truck was parked directly beside hers, with a horse trailer attached. Closing her eyes, she released a long sigh of relief.

"What did you think—" she whirled at the sound of Cord's voice "—that I'd take off running after we tied the knot?"

"Cord!" She grasped the pillow tightly to her. "You scared me half to death."

His form was no more than a shadow in the corner of the room where he'd been sitting in an armchair. When he rose and moved toward her, she had to resist stepping back. She noticed he'd changed back into jeans and a clean, white shirt. His hat was on the table beside the chair.

"You didn't answer my question."

"Well," she said, glancing back at the parking lot. "It crossed my mind for a moment."

She moved to switch on the light, but he took hold of her arm, stopping her. With his other hand, he took the pillow from her and tossed it on the bed. She knew she should be frightened, alone in a dark hotel room with a man she didn't know, her *husband,* no less, but she wasn't afraid. She could feel the heavy thudding of her heart, feel the heat of his hand on her arm, and the only thing she was afraid of was herself.

"I thought about it, Rachel," he said, running his hand down her arm and taking her hand. "I'd be lying if I didn't admit that this marriage business scares the hell out of me."

Cord saw the surprise in Rachel's sleep-laden eyes. The lights from the parking lot illuminated her pale face and tousled hair. He glanced down at their clasped hands, noting how small her fingers were in his palm, how warm her skin was. When he turned her hand over in his, the gold band winked at him.

He'd come close to leaving. After he'd packed up his things and gotten his horses loaded, he'd felt freer than he had in a long time. The call to drive north, maybe back up to Montana, had been strong.

And then he'd thought about Rachel sleeping in this hotel room, trusting him, waiting for him to come back, and he'd turned south.

"You can still change your mind," she said softly. "I won't hold you to this…arrangement…if you want out."

Her voice, throaty and seductive, stirred his blood. Here he was, asking her if she trusted him, when he didn't even trust himself. He released her hand and stepped away, turning on the light.

"We have an agreement, partner," he said in his heaviest Texas drawl. The sight of her in her stocking feet, her skirt rumpled and her blouse unbuttoned at the top made his throat constrict. "There's no turning back now, darlin'. What's the expression…?" He grinned slowly. "We've made our bed, now we gotta lie in it."

She blushed at his analogy. "Figuratively speaking, of course."

"Of course."

"Cord," she said tentatively, glancing down at her hand, "I want to thank you for the ring. I hadn't expected one."

The soft look in her eyes brought a lump to his throat. He swallowed it back and shrugged. "Well, it wouldn't look too good if you didn't have one. We sure don't want people to talk, do we?"

She laughed. "I doubt there's any way around that, but I suppose that's one fire we don't need to add any fuel to, either. Considering the circumstances, we'll be at bonfire proportions before the sun sets tomorrow night."

They both smiled.

"Why didn't you wake me?" she asked. "We could have been home by now."

Home. It wasn't a word he was used to hearing. His skin suddenly felt too tight. He moved to the window and looked out at the parking lot, at his truck. "I doubt an explosion would have woke you up, Rachel. I made enough noise to wake the dead when I came in, and you never budged."

He turned back to her. "It's been a long day for me, too, and I'd like to get something to eat then grab some shut-eye. I've already told the front desk we'll need the room another night. Tomorrow morning will be soon enough to leave."

Tomorrow morning? Sleep in the same room? Rachel looked at the double bed, then back to Cord. "Uh, well . . . okay. I've really had enough sleep anyway, and I don't need the bed anymore, so if you want to use it, you can." She scratched nervously at the back of her neck. "I can just curl up in the chair and . . . read, or something."

It had been a long time since Cord had been around a woman who blushed. He found it intriguing, as well as enticing. The fact that she was offering her bed to him, even though she was obviously in need of a good night's sleep herself, was equally charming. He looked over at the rumpled blanket and the image of her lying there, wearing something silky and lacy—like a real bride—sparked a fire in his blood. Even if he took her up on her offer, there'd be no way he'd get any sleep in that bed. He'd smell the sweet scent of her, know she was only a few feet away, and sleep would be the farthest thing from his mind.

Besides, he looked back at Rachel and saw the tension in her face, she just might lose her stomach again if he said yes. He wasn't sure whether he should be amused, or annoyed by that thought.

"Thanks for the offer," he said, gesturing to his truck, "but I'll have to tie the horses behind the hotel, so I'll be sleeping in the trailer tonight."

Rachel walked to the window and looked out. "We could have picked them up in the morning."

"Well—" Cord raked a hand through his dark hair "—my ex-boss was somewhat perturbed with me for leaving so sudden and he was downright candid about where 'me and my animals could go.'"

Cord thought it best not to mention that his breaking every whip on the Bar None was what had really angered the other man. Cord's only regret was that he hadn't broken every last whip over that bastard's head.

"So," he said, reaching for his hat on the table by the chair, "let's say we rustle up some chow and hit the hay." He glanced at his horse trailer and smiled. "Literally speaking."

Rachel laughed. "Seems like all you've done is feed me since we got married, Mr. Cantrell. I'm going to get fat if you keep this up."

Rachel slipped on a pair of flats and straightened her clothes and Cord was disturbingly reminded that feeding her was not all he wanted to do. But a bargain was a bargain, he thought almost painfully as she slipped on her jacket and he noticed her breasts press tightly against the thin silk of her blouse.

At least—he held the door open and caught her light flowery scent as she walked past him —a bargain was a bargain until both parties agreed it wasn't.

Rachel packed her clothes early the next morning while Cord showered. After spending a restless night worrying about how she was going to explain her sudden marriage, she was tired, irritable and anxious. Of course, she'd known that she'd have to come up with a story if she did find a husband, but now that she actually had one, she was at a loss for words. Eyebrows and questions were bound to rise.

"So where did you meet?" she asked herself out loud, pretending she was one of the ranch hands.

Good question. Everyone thought she'd gone to Dallas on business for a few days. She tapped her chin while she thought about an answer.

"An auction in Dallas." That sounded plausible. Especially since Earl had fired her last trainer. It would only make sense she'd be interested in meeting a new one. *Marrying one,* however, was an entirely different story. She'd just keep her answers short, she decided. There'd be less opportunity of slipping up.

"And you got married after only four days?" she asked herself incredulously.

"It was love at first sight," she cooed. "We just couldn't help ourselves."

Oh, sure, they'll really buy that one. Moaning softly, Rachel shook her head. How was she ever going to pull this off? It was going to be blatantly obvious to everyone they weren't in love.

The only thing to be thankful for, she told herself, was the fact that Earl would be in California for another week. She knew he'd stop by the ranch on his way home—a fancy condo in Fort Worth he moved into after his third divorce. She had no idea how Earl was going to react to her marriage, but she knew it would not be good. With a sigh, she folded the suit she'd worn yesterday and laid it in the suitcase. Her fingertips hesitated as she smoothed out the wrinkles.

She glanced at the bathroom door, heard the shower running and an image of pulsating water on broad, muscled shoulders crept into her mind. Her heart picked up its pace. When her imagination decided to expand and define, Rachel quickly put a halt to her thoughts.

She was attracted to Cord, Rachel reluctantly admitted. What woman wouldn't be? But getting involved with him beyond their business agreement was out of the question. She loved her independence, not having to answer to anyone. A woman could too easily lose herself in a relationship and think with her heart or her body instead of her head. She had a ranch at stake here and that was all that mattered to her.

Besides, she thought, tucking her heels into her suitcase, Cord would be leaving in a year and she just wasn't the type for a casual affair. She'd had plenty of offers since Michael's death, and even an offer or two before, she remembered with distaste, but she wanted no complications, nothing to tie her down. At least, not until the ranch was running smoothly again. Then she'd think about marriage and children. She smiled at that thought. A ranch like the Circle T begged for a passel of kids.

In the meantime, there was no reason why she and Cord couldn't get along for that short period of time. Be friends. She refused to allow her attraction to him to interfere with her plans. Surely she could manage to avoid him for one measly year. She had a big house, Cord would be working, she would be working. They'd probably never even see each other. A year would fly by in a snap.

When the shower stopped, she heard Cord whistling softly while he toweled off. Suddenly the door opened and he stuck out his head and half his body. "You have any toothpaste?" he asked. "I forgot mine." His black hair, shiny when wet, was combed straight back. Water dripped down his forehead and neck. Steam billowed out of the bathroom behind him and he was holding a towel around his hips. Rachel refused to allow her gaze to drift farther than his glistening shoulders.

Her hand shook as she pulled her toiletries bag out of her suitcase and dug a tube from the bottom. She tossed it to him, never really meeting his eyes, and when he closed the bathroom door again she let out a sigh of relief.

Toothpaste. He'd asked to use her toothpaste as calmly as if they actually were married. Well, married like regular people, she added. The idea of him using her toothpaste brought a silly quivering sensation in the pit of her stomach. She knew it was just her nerves making her feel this way, but still she was suddenly glad they were driving separately and she'd have the next three hours to be alone. Three hours to calm her nerves and decide exactly how she was going to explain Mr. Cord Cantrell.

Fifteen minutes later they were checked out and on the road. Two hours after that they stopped for a drive-through lunch and to water the horses, then one hour after that Rachel turned onto the road that led to the Circle T. Behind her, in a cloud of dust, Cord followed.

Home. It was like a strong shot of whiskey. She felt warm inside, choked up. She suddenly knew, without a doubt, that what she'd done was right. No matter what else happened, saving this ranch was truly the only important thing to her.

Unable to contain her excitement, she pulled off to the side and cut the engine. Smiling, she jumped from the truck and ran over to Cord, who was parking behind her.

"Come on, cowboy," she said, pulling open the door of his truck before he even shut the engine off. "I'm going to show you what a real ranch looks like."

Rachel's enthusiasm surprised Cord. He'd always thought her reserved, composed. Certainly not one to cut loose with such an open display of emotion. He immediately decided he liked this side of her. In spite of the drain of a long drive, her eyes were bright, her cheeks flushed with excitement. And her smile, as generous as it was spontaneous, enchanted him, infected him, until he found himself smiling back, already delighting in whatever it was she wanted to show him.

He stepped out of the truck—or rather, was dragged out by Rachel's insistent hand—and looked around.

"Isn't it beautiful?" she whispered. She let go of his arm and walked several feet away, then turned slowly in a circle as she took it all in.

It was open range as far as the eye could see. Scrub, sagebrush, scattered oak trees. Tipping his hat back, he glanced up at the sky, a deep blue, laced in the distance with thin puffs of clouds.

"Look!" She pointed a finger at a hawk as it swooped low over a potential meal, then soared upward, its claws empty. "See what I mean?" she said, turning back to him.

He didn't. It was a nice piece of property, but it looked pretty much like any other ranch he'd ever seen. Maybe Rachel hadn't been around much, he thought. The novelty was still new to her.

"It's nice," he said.

Rachel stared at him, frowning. Hands on her hips, she walked up to him. "It's better than nice," she said with an intensity that raised Cord's brows. "It's mine. And as soon as I get rid of Earl, no one, and nobody, is going to tell me how to run it."

She spun on her heels and climbed back into her truck, taking off with a roar that sent the back wheels spinning dirt and gravel. Bewildered, Cord watched her drive off, wondering what in the world had gotten into her. Shaking his head, he climbed back into his truck and followed. Would he ever figure women out? Women, hell. Right now he'd be happy if he could understand just one.

She'd been unusually quiet after they'd checked out of the hotel and gone to breakfast. Their only conversation had been when she'd asked him to let her handle the introductions and explanations when they got to the ranch. He'd agreed and she'd barely said another word other than that. She'd seemed...tense. Not that he couldn't understand that. After all, she was bringing a strange man home, he thought, then smiled at his own choice of words. But he sensed there was more to her uneasiness than the obvious. Something he couldn't quite put his finger on.

In the distance, about a quarter mile up the dirt road, Cord spotted a house, Spanish-style, with a red tile roof and arched entryway. The house was long and rambling, surrounded by live oaks and green lawn. He noticed the stables and two riding rings several hundred feet beyond, plus a scattering of small cabins that probably housed the help.

Rachel waved an arm out of her truck, signaling for him to park in front of the house. As he pulled up beside her, she stepped out of her pickup.

"Just come in for a minute," she said, walking over to him. "Then I'll ride down to the stables with you and help you get your horses settled."

Cord shut the engine off and followed her up the tiled walk leading to the entry. A basket of fragrant yellow flowers caught his attention. Just like a real home, he thought. At least, what he'd imagined a real home would be like.

Rachel turned to him at the front door and smiled hesitantly. "I've had Judy, my foreman's wife, take care of things here for me while I've been gone, but she'll probably be back at her house fixing dinner now, so we should be alone."

Cord realized she was trying to say that they wouldn't have to be explaining who he was to anyone just yet. In fact, he had the distinct feeling she stopped at the house just to gather up that last bit of courage before they went to the stables and encountered her ranch hands. The blushing bride, he thought with amusement, noting the color in her cheeks. As she opened the front door, an irresistible impulse grabbed hold of him.

She gasped as he scooped her up in his arms.

"Cord! What are you doing?"

He grinned. Her eyes were wide, her lips parted in shock. "Why, just carrying my wife over the threshold," he teased, kicking the door wider open with the toe of his boot. Damn if those curves of hers didn't feel as good as they looked, he thought, stepping into the house.

Rachel laughed nervously. "Cord, really, you don't have to do this, it's not as if—"

He cut her words off by closing his mouth over hers.

Four

She couldn't move. His lips claimed hers so suddenly, with such insistency, she was paralyzed. But only for a moment. His kiss opened a floodgate of feelings within her and they poured through her: shock, excitement, fear. And desire. It had been so long since a man had held her in his arms—since she'd wanted a man to hold her. There was no logic in this, she knew, only a reckless need that made her heart pound wildly and her breath ragged. Even as she tightened her arm around his shoulders, she called herself a fool.

Still holding her in his arms, Cord kicked the door shut, then slowly lowered her, letting her body slide down the hard length of him until her toes touched the floor. Passion sparked between them. From the first time she'd met him she'd known it would be like this with him. Wild and careless. Untamed.

He whispered something incoherent, then pressed her against the door, cupping her bottom in his large hands and lifting her to fit intimately to him. His arousal excited her, yet frightened her. He was moving too fast. She started to push away, but he pulled her tighter and slanted his mouth roughly against hers, deepening the kiss, turning up the heat that was already whipping through her. She'd never been kissed like this, never experienced such abandon. Her arms wound around his neck, knocking his hat carelessly to the floor. She pressed against him, needing to be closer, wanting so badly to understand this strange passion, but terrified at the same time.

From the first exotic taste of her lips, Cord had forgotten his original intention. He'd never dreamed she'd respond like this, that she would be so soft, so sweet. So willing. He held her firmly to him, resisting the urge to move against her the way his body craved. Her arms tightened around him. He felt, rather than heard, the low moan from her throat. Dammit! He was losing control and he couldn't allow that. Not now.

Not with someone watching.

The loud clearing of a deep, male voice made Rachel freeze. She realized with startling clarity that she and Cord were not alone. For a moment she felt angry at the intrusion, then, as reality slowly came back to her senses, she gripped Cord's shoulders in panic.

In spite of their unexpected visitor, Cord felt reluctant to let Rachel go. Her green eyes, still dark with passion, met his briefly, then looked over his shoulder. "Easy, babe," he whispered, straightening slowly. "We've got company."

She paled, then her face flushed beet red. Casually, Cord turned and followed the direction of her gaze. Standing in a doorway, ten feet away from them, was a tall man with thinning brown hair. The expression on his deeply tanned face was fierce, angry. His heavy brows were drawn, his arms folded tightly across his wide chest. The stance was a deliberate attempt to intimidate. He looked as if he owned the place, and Rachel, too.

Cord didn't like that look.

Without being told, there was no doubt in Cord's mind that this was the brother-in-law, Earl, who had driven Rachel to find a husband. From what she'd told him, he was penny-pinching her ranch into bankruptcy, but it was obvious he was not a man who skimped on himself. He looked as if he'd just stepped out of a men's fashion catalog. Pressed white shirt, tan slacks, polished dress shoes. The diamond rings he wore on his manicured hands would probably pay for five years' hay and feed alone.

Instinct tightened the muscles at the back of Cord's neck and had him slipping an arm around Rachel's shoulders as he turned and faced the other man.

"Earl." Rachel combed her hair back with shaky fingers. "I—I thought you were still in California."

"Obviously." Earl's gaze locked with Cord's.

A moment of silence stretched on to what seemed like an eternity to Rachel. This was all happening too fast. She still hadn't recovered from the roller-coaster kiss that Cord had just given her, and now she had to face Earl and explain her sudden marriage.

A thousand butterflies took wing in her stomach as Earl moved into the entry. He'd see right through her. She knew it. He'd know why she married Cord and, like the bulldog he was, he'd hold on and fight to retain control. Of all the things that Earl was, he was not a quitter.

But neither was she. Not anymore.

She drew in a fortifying breath and straightened her shoulders. *Stay calm. Be in control.* Michael had taught her that.

She forced an effervescent smile and wrapped her arms around Cord's waist. "Earl, I want you to meet Cord Cantrell." She swallowed hard. "My husband."

Rachel watched the gradual dawning of comprehension on Earl's harsh features. Astonishment slowly faded to anger. "What?" he asked sharply.

"We were married yesterday." Rachel laid a hand on Cord's chest, revealing the gold band. The solid, strong thud of his heart helped steady her trembling fingers.

"Married!" Earl spat the word. "I've only been gone a week and you're *married?*" His gaze hardened as he glanced at Cord. "To *him?*"

The way Earl said "him" made it sound like something you'd step on before it crawled away. Tension bunched in Cord's muscles beneath her damp palms.

"Earl, it's really not necessary to—"

"Rachel," he said, cutting her off, "I'd like to have a word with you in the office." Without waiting for her to answer, he turned.

Rachel pressed her lips tightly together. Though it galled her, not only because he'd said "the office," instead of "your office," but because he'd assumed she'd follow. But then, isn't that what she'd always done? She closed her eyes and let out a long breath. Maybe it would be better if she talked to Earl in private. The murderous look in Cord's eyes was only going to lead to trouble. What she didn't need right now were two bulls stomping and snorting at each other.

She moved away from Cord and started after Earl. Cord reached out and pulled her back. His hand on her arm was firm. Possessive.

"Mr. Stephens."

The deadly calm in Cord's voice stopped Earl. He turned slowly, his gaze narrowed.

"Whatever you have to say—" Cord pulled Rachel against him "—you can say it out here."

She shot a glance at Cord, careful not to give in to the frown pushing at her lips. They would hardly appear to be the "happy couple" if she were glaring. She bit the inside of her mouth. Dammit, anyway! Why were men so hell-bent on having things their way?

Earl walked back into the entry. "You move fast, mister." His face was dark with fury. "Did you talk her into this before, or after, you found out who she was?"

Cord went still. He tightened his grip on Rachel's shoulder, then slowly dropped his arm as he moved to take a step toward Earl. She gritted her teeth, furious that she was stuck in the middle of this power-play between Cord and Earl. She'd told Cord she'd wanted to handle it her own way, but no, macho man that he was, he just *had* to do it his way.

She placed a hand on Cord's chest. The anger she felt radiating off of him made her fingers jump. "Cord, please."

His gaze was cold, his jaw set as he continued to look at Earl. "Who she *is,*" Cord said tightly, "is *my* wife. I think it might be best if you remember that before we continue this discussion."

A hard glint shone in Earl's eyes. He pressed his lips together, obviously biting back his own anger. He shifted his attention to Rachel. "You can hardly blame me for being surprised, Rachel. We've been family for so long now, your...news...has left me somewhat stunned." He softened his expression. "Since Michael's death, your welfare has always been my foremost concern."

It was hard to hold back the laugh. Rachel knew the only "welfare" that concerned Earl, was his own. And the bottom line of a financial statement. What he was doing, she realized, was changing tactics. When intimidation didn't work, he always appealed to her emotions. Soon he'd be launching into his "I'm only doing what Michael would want" speech.

"I appreciate your concern, Earl," she said evenly. "And I'm sorry I wasn't able to contact you. It's just that it...happened so fast." A muscle twitched in Cord's jaw when she apologized. There was no way Earl was going to listen to one word she had to say with Cord scowling like he was.

"Cord, honey." She turned to him, plastering a smile on her lips. She watched his gaze narrow at her use of the endearment. "I know you have to get the horses settled. Would you mind if I stayed here and talked to Earl? Sam, my—our—foreman, can give you a hand and I'll be down in a few minutes."

Cord's eyes turned the color of a stormy sea. "Why, sure, darlin'." His face lost all expression. "I might as well go out and meet the rest of the hired help."

Rachel flinched at Cord's words. She hadn't meant to patronize him, but she doubted he'd believe that right now. His hand was tight on her shoulder as he pulled her against him and planted a stiff kiss on her lips. He released her, retrieved his hat from the floor, then shot a hard look at Earl. "Mr. Stephens." He settled his hat on his head.

Rachel watched Cord close the door behind him. She wanted to follow, to explain, but Earl had moved beside her and taken her arm.

"Are you all right?" He squeezed her hand. "You look a little pale."

All right? she thought, glancing down at his cold hand on hers. She clenched her jaw, resisting the urge to break out in laughter. *I'm married to a man I've known exactly four days just so I can get rid of you, and you ask me if I'm all right?*

"Of course I'm all right." She looked at the door Cord had just walked through. "I'm a little tired, that's all."

Earl took her shoulders in his hands and turned her to face him. "Rachel," he said, his expression grim, "I want you to tell me, and I want the truth. Why did you really marry that man?"

Cord pulled his truck and trailer beside the stables, jammed the gear shift into park and cut the engine. He felt like a damn fool. A damn *stupid* fool. He gritted his teeth, trying to figure out what had gotten into him back at the house. Only a few hours ago he'd agreed to let Rachel handle the explanations, but the minute Earl had opened his mouth, something just short-circuited. He shook his head with disgust. Sir Galahad to the rescue.

Some rescue.

All that his gallantry had gotten him from Rachel was a dismissal. A polite one perhaps, but a dismissal just the same. As if he were an employee who'd forgotten his place.

But then, wasn't that what he was? And he *had* forgotten his place, kissing Rachel had certainly proven that.

When they'd stepped into the entry and he'd realized that someone was standing there, he'd kissed her to stop her from blurting out that they really weren't married. Her response was something he hadn't counted on. The woman was pure passion, and Lord, she tasted sweet. Sweeter than he'd ever remembered another woman tasting. And softer. When she'd pressed up against him he'd nearly lost it completely. Like a wild bronco, he'd held on for the ride, never wanting it to end.

He cursed that idiot Earl for being there. For interrupting. But then, if Earl hadn't been there, Cord realized, he wouldn't have kissed Rachel. All the more reason to dislike Earl. Now that Cord knew the heat simmering beneath Rachel's calm exterior, how could he keep his hands off of her?

"Can I help you with something, cowboy?"

Cord started at the sound of the gravelly voice. An elderly man with a thick head of silver-gray hair and a deeply creased face stood outside the truck. "You can if your name's Sam."

The old man looked Cord over. "Less'n you're looking for a loan, or repayment of one, that's me."

Cord smiled and stepped out of the truck. He extended his hand. "Cord Cantrell. Rachel told me to ask for you so I can get my horses settled in."

Sam's heavy brows rose as he accepted Cord's hand. "You hired on?"

"Something like that."

The foreman followed Cord to the back of the trailer. "Name sounds familiar," Sam said, scratching the back of his head. The old man's eyes grew wide. "Cord Cantrell! I remember now. Why, you done near won the Fort Worth Futurity last year. I seen you ride that sorrel gelding of yours—what's his name?"

"Montana Moon." Cord flipped open the trailer gate.

"Yeah! Montana Moon." The old man broke into a wide grin. "You rode that horse like the devil hisself!"

Smiling at the comparison, Cord stepped into the trailer, slipped a halter onto Montana, then led him out. Sam whistled appreciatively and grabbed hold of the lead. "Whooee! Ain't he a pretty one!"

Next came Cord's most recent purchase, her registered name being Sassafras Lady, but he'd decided to simply call her Lady.

After watering them, Sam put the horses on the hot walker to stretch their legs, then showed Cord two empty stalls he could use. While Cord rebedded the stalls with fresh pine shaving, Sam chattered on. In the middle of the foreman's lengthy reminiscing of the previous year's Fort Worth Futurity, Rachel walked into the stable. Cord noted the strained look on her face, then dismissed the renewed surge of anger he felt toward Earl. She'd wanted to handle it her way. Fine. She was the boss.

"Hi, Sam."

Sam turned at the sound of Rachel's voice and touched the brim of his hat. "Welcome back, Miz Stephens. I was just setting Cord up here in the stable while his horses are stretching their legs on the walker."

And talking his ear off, Rachel realized, smiling. "Thanks, Sam. I appreciate it."

The foreman nodded. "By the way, if you haven't already made plans for the boy, I'd sure be happy to have him bunk in with Judy and me. We've got that spare bedroom since you gave my boys their own place."

Sam happy to have someone bunk with him? How could Cord have made that big an impression in such a short period of time? But then, she remembered reluctantly, she'd also been impressed with their first meeting. For different reasons, she'd nearly had the same thought about "bunking" with Cord.

She glanced at Cord, slightly annoyed that he hadn't told Sam about them. Obviously, he was intentionally trying to make things difficult for her after she'd asked him indirectly to leave her alone with Earl. She sighed inwardly. Not that it mattered now. If she could survive telling Earl, she could certainly survive breaking the news to Sam, though she knew that with her foreman's loose jaw everyone within a hundred-mile radius would be informed before the hour was up.

"Actually, I have made plans for Mr. Cantrell." Rachel held Cord's steady gaze. "He'll be sleeping at the main house." Sam's jaw dropped. "Also, Sam, you'll need to get used to calling me Mrs. Cantrell now. As of yesterday, Cord is my husband."

It was probably the first time Rachel had ever seen Sam speechless. Eyes wide, he looked at Cord, then pointed an accusing finger. "And here you let me ramble on, Mr. Cantrell, like you was just one of the hands."

"The name is Cord, Sam, and I don't want you to think of me as anything but one of the hands." He lifted the rake he'd been leaning against in a silent salute to Rachel.

So he *was* still mad, she realized, pursing her lips. As if it hadn't been bad with Earl, now she had to deal with Cord's obstinacy. "I'd like to show my husband around the Circle T, Sam. Would you please find Parker and ask him to clear a spot for Cord's tack?"

"Do it myself," Sam said cheerfully and strode bow-legged out of the barn.

Two miracles in one day, Rachel thought, noting the enthusiasm in Sam's step. Sam speechless, and Sam happy to do grunt work. Something very strange was going on here.

Shaking her head, she turned back to Cord. He set the rake down, then dumped a wheelbarrow full of shavings into the second stall and began spreading it. He hadn't given her a second glance.

"Are these stalls all right with you?" she asked, hoping to get a conversation going.

"Fine."

He'd rolled his shirtsleeves to his elbows and she watched his muscles bunch and relax as he worked the rake. His hat was tipped back and from the look of intense concentration on his face she'd have thought he'd entered a raking competition.

Exasperated, she picked up a second rake and started to help. "So what do you think of Sam?"

"I like him." He cast her a sideways glance, but never hesitated in his work.

Damn the man! Couldn't he see she was trying to make amends here? No, of course he couldn't. He was still too wrapped up in his own ego. Sighing, Rachel straightened. "Cord, aren't you going to ask me what happened with Earl?"

She watched him stiffen and his jaw went tight, but he kept on working. "It's not my job to ask questions. You got a horse to train, or a stall to clean, just give me a whistle, otherwise, I'll mind my own business."

She slammed the rake down and put her hands on her hips. "Look, Cord, I realize you've had your male pride bruised by what happened at the house and I'm sorry about that, but I've had my quota today of stubborn, arrogant men. When you're ready to talk about it, I'll be at the house."

She'd never dreamed a man could move so fast. She hadn't even turned before he grabbed her arm and whipped her around. "You want to talk about it? Fine," he said, his eyes blazing with anger. "I'll tell you what's bothering me, *Mrs. Cantrell*. Whether this is a *real* marriage or not, you *are* my wife. That means something to me, even if it doesn't to you. The thought of leaving you alone with that pompous SOB made me want to rip something apart, preferably that idiot brother-in-law of yours."

She started to pull away from him, but his words stopped her. Why would he be upset about her being alone with Earl? "I thought you were mad because...well, because I—"

"Asked me to leave?" he finished for her. He eased his grip on her arm, but didn't let go. "It made me mad as hell." The tautness of his body relaxed noticeably, but the strain in his eyes lingered. "But I also know I had it coming. You'd asked me to let you handle it your way and I'd agreed. Until I met Earl."

Rachel understood that Earl could easily make a person crazy. "That's exactly why I needed you out of there, Cord. You had a look in your eyes that said you were about ready to turn Earl into a human pretzel." She smiled. "And though that thought is not entirely distasteful to me, I've got to be careful until I have control of my trust and the Circle T is actually in my hands. If I make him angry, he'll stall as long as it takes. The Circle T doesn't have that kind of time. We're barely getting by."

Cord knew that what she was saying was true. It didn't appear she had nearly enough horses to bring in the kind of money required to run a spread this big. He'd also noticed the bedding was inferior and the barn was in need of repair. What he didn't understand was why it was so important to Rachel. "So you'll buy another ranch if the Circle T doesn't make it. Once you get rid of Earl, you can live anywhere you want."

A bell rang somewhere in the distance and Rachel turned her head at the sound. She smiled slowly. "You know what that is?" she asked, looking back into Cord's eyes.

He shook his head. "What?"

"That's Judy calling Sam and their two sons, Clint and Dave, to dinner. Every day she threatens if they're late they'll be eating cold beans out with the chickens, but they all know they could come in at midnight and there'd be a hot meal on the table."

Her voice had softened, and she had a dreamy, distant look on her face. "The Circle T *is* what I want, Cord. The dirt and dust and heat, the blue sky and open spaces. All of it, the good and the bad." She lifted her gaze to his and the determination shone in her gray-green eyes. "I want to raise my children here, give them all the things I never had, things that can't be bought. A home, a real home, not a string of temporary residences made of cold walls and empty rooms."

An image flashed in Cord's mind of Rachel standing on a porch, clanging away at some silly bell, smiling as a little boy with dark hair came racing home for supper.

Feelings that Cord had thought long dead began to stir. He wrestled them back down, refusing to allow them life. The image vanished, but the reality didn't. Her skin was warm and soft beneath his fingers and he felt a slow burn creep through his body. The need to pull her into his arms overwhelmed him. He stared at the tempting white skin of her long slender neck, watched her pulse flicker, then speed up. When she looked up at him he knew she felt it, too. He could see the need shimmer in her eyes.

"Cord." Her voice was ragged. "I'd appreciate it if you let go of me."

He leaned closer. Her hair smelled like spring flowers. "That's not what you said earlier, when I carried you over the threshold."

Rachel fought the urge to close the sliver of space between them. She hadn't forgotten that kiss. She doubted she ever would. She just had to make sure it didn't happen again. "We agreed I wasn't part of this arrangement."

Smiling, he brought his lips close to hers. "I assure you, it wasn't personal."

"What?" She stilled beneath him.

"I did it to shut you up." He wanted to shut her up again. Right now. To sink his hands in her hair and kiss her until she felt the same ache he did. With will-power he didn't know he possessed, Cord dropped his hand and moved away. ''I realized there was someone standing there when we walked in. You were about to say we really weren't married. I acted instinctively, but it was strictly business, I assure you.''

Strictly business? She felt a tingle shoot up her spine just thinking about that kiss and how she'd re-sponded. And the only reason he'd done it was to shut her up? Her cheeks grew warm.

''The next time will be different, though,'' he said, bending down to pick up the rake she'd thrown in frustration.

''Next time?'' Confused, she watched him lean to-ward her as he straightened.

''I kiss you,'' he said so close to her ear his breath fanned her neck. ''The next time, there won't be any-one there and I promise you—'' her breath held as his lips stopped a fraction of an inch from her earlobe ''—it won't be business.''

There was just no getting rid of her brother-in-law, Rachel thought dismally as she cleared the dinner dishes from the dining room table. Earl had insisted on staying to share a congratulatory meal with the newlyweds, but she knew his motives went much deeper. He'd been sizing Cord up, casually asking questions about who he was and where he was from. He'd also asked Cord questions she'd already an-swered this afternoon. Like how she and Cord had met and where they'd gotten married. It was as if he were trying to trip them up somehow. Earl was suspicious, of that she was sure, and she was glad that she and Cord had gotten their stories straight. At least the two men had stayed in their own corners throughout the meal—a hastily thrown-together casserole and salad.

For what seemed like the hundredth time, she looked at the clock, worrying that if Earl didn't leave soon, he just might decide to stay the night rather than drive back to Dallas.

The thought made her hurry and she dumped the dishes into the sink, then turned to the coffeepot. The smell almost choked her. Earl had said he needed a good strong dose of caffeine for the drive home, so she'd nearly tripled the usual measurement and set it to brew before they ate. One cup ought to do it and then he'd be on his way. She filled three mugs, wrinkling her nose at the thick consistency. That ought to take care of old Earl, she thought with a satisfied nod.

"So last year," Rachel heard Earl say to Cord, "I invested in this chemical company that's about to become a virtual gold mine. Michael had been looking into it before he died, but—"

Cord turned his attention away from Earl's rambling and watched Rachel move into the dining room, carefully maneuvering three mugs of steaming coffee. At the mention of Michael's name, her lips had drawn into a thin line. He'd noticed she'd tensed every time Michael's name was mentioned this evening. And that had been several times. When Earl hadn't been asking personal questions regarding Cord's background, he'd been bragging about his business coups or talking about Michael. Cord had figured out that Earl had decided to kill him with boredom.

"Speaking of investments," Rachel interrupted as she sat down at the table, "I was wondering where my check is for the month. I'm going to be late on the mortgage again and the shoer is coming this week."

Earl took a quick sip of coffee and coughed. He wiped at his mouth with a napkin. "I drew up a check before I went to California. Didn't you get it?"

She'd heard that one before. "No."

"Damn, it's hard to find a decent secretary these days," he grumbled. "Well, consider it handled tomorrow. I'll be at the office first thing in the morning and I'll have it expressed to you."

She'd heard *that* one before, too. "I could drive in and pick it up," she suggested. "It might be a good time for us to discuss my assumption of the trust." She smiled sweetly. "I wouldn't consider burdening you with that job anymore. I know it's taken a considerable amount of time away from your own responsibilities."

"Don't be silly, Rachel." His tone was ingratiating. "You know I've never minded. You would have been lost in the complexities of Michael's affairs, that's why he wanted it this way."

Michael again. Rachel resisted the frown. "Actually—" she held her mug between her hands and looked Earl in the eye "—I've decided to sell everything but the ranch."

Rachel noticed an exaggerated calm in Earl's movements as he dared a second sip of coffee. He choked slightly, then frowned at the cup. "Is this a new brand you're using, Rachel? I don't recall your coffee having such a bite."

"Sorry about that, Earl," Cord said. "Rachel made it the way I like it. I can get some milk for you if it'll help."

Surprised, Rachel glanced at Cord. He lifted his mug to her and took a big swallow. She couldn't resist smiling back.

"It's fine." As if to prove it, Earl took another sip. He looked as if he were drinking mud. He turned his attention back to her. "I've explained to you already that all your money is tied up in real estate. With the market down the way it is, it would be foolish to sell right now."

"Maybe so," Rachel said, holding Earl's disapproving gaze, "but it is my decision, foolish or not."

Earl's sigh was patronizing. "Rachel, you'd be taking a tremendous loss on that property. Now if you'd change your mind and sell the ranch, I already have a buyer who's willing to pay top dollar."

Her fingers tightened around the handle of her coffee mug. "We've been through this before, Earl. I'm not selling the ranch," she said firmly. "I don't care what my losses are on the other property. The Circle T is all that matters to me."

Earl leaned forward, his tone angry. "You're willing to lose a great deal of the trust left to you in order to hold on to a broken-down, money-sucking horse ranch. What kind of business sense is that?" He placed both palms on the table and leaned forward. "That's exactly why Michael left your trust in my hands. Without someone looking after you, it won't be long before you have nothing."

"She has someone looking out for her."

Rachel turned at Cord's words, issued with an icy calmness that belied the fierce expression in his eyes. Cord's shoulders were stiff as he leaned back in his chair. "She has me, Stephens. I suggest you remember that."

There was a split second of pure male challenge between the two men that made Rachel glad she'd already cleared the table of utensils.

"Well, of course she does, Cord," Earl said through gritted teeth. "But with all due respect, what do you know about business? Training horses is not exactly what's considered high finance."

"Maybe not," Cord drawled. "But I learned enough to know when to hire someone if I can't do the job myself. It's as simple as opening the phone book. Accountant starts with *A* and lawyer with *L*."

Earl's face darkened. "Is that some kind of a threat, Cantrell?"

"Of course it's not," Rachel cut in. This conversation was quickly getting out of hand and she needed to stop it now before fists started swinging. "Cord just knows how anxious I am to handle my own affairs. I'd appreciate it if you could get the paperwork together for me, Earl. It's been two years, and since I am married now, there's no reason to hold off any longer."

"Very well, then." Earl's expression was stony. "I'll start the ball in motion as soon as I get back to my office tomorrow." He glanced at his watch, took one last swallow of coffee and stood. "And if I want to be there bright and early, I'd better get going. I've got a meeting in the morning and—" A low rumble in the distance cut off his words.

Thunder.

No. It couldn't be. Not tonight, of all nights. Rachel hurried to the living room window just in time to see a bolt of lightning streak through the black Texas night. A second rumble shook the windows. Winds whipped the brush and trees in the yard. Her stomach clenched. Earl moved beside her.

"A storm's moving in fast." From the tone of his voice, Rachel realized that Earl was no happier about it than she was. He turned from the window and said tightly, "Hope you two don't mind, but it looks like I'll be spending the night."

Mind? Earl couldn't stay the night. He couldn't. She threw Cord a frantic look and didn't miss the amusement in his eyes. He'd already figured out her predicament. A scream bubbled at the base of her throat.

She and Cord were going to have to sleep in the same bedroom.

Five

It was a hot storm. A violent downpour that charged the air with electricity and filled Rachel's lungs with the fresh, clean scent of rain. Under normal circumstances, she would have welcomed this kind of storm enthusiastically. Not only because the rain was needed, but because she'd always felt a sense of contentment and inner peace being tucked safely inside while a storm raged around her.

She hesitated in her unpacking. *Normal circumstances?* She would have laughed at that thought if her throat didn't feel so dry and her stomach wasn't churning. The word *normal* simply did not apply to her life.

Not since she'd met Cord Cantrell.

She glanced over at the open French doors that led to the patio outside her bedroom. Cord stood with his back to her, his arms folded, staring out into the black

Texas night. The only light in the room was from a small bedside lamp she'd turned on when she'd come in after situating Earl in the guest room. If she'd been alone, she'd have left the room dark and watched the storm for hours.

Rain pounded the metal awning over the patio. She watched, mesmerized, as a gust of warm air swept in and caught the ends of Cord's dark hair, then held her breath when a sudden flash of lightning silhouetted his lean, muscular body in the doorway. Thunder shook the windows.

He was beautiful. Like a wild stallion corralled for the first time. It gave her no pleasure that she was the one who had slipped the bridle on him, however temporary it was. While being married would solve many of her problems, she had the uneasy feeling she was creating a bigger, and perhaps more dangerous one.

"Rachel."

She jumped when he called her name. She had a fleeting, uncanny feeling that he'd been listening to her thoughts. He turned from the doors, his brow furrowed.

"Yes?"

"How well do you know Earl?"

Why would he ask her a question like that? She paused and met Cord's thoughtful gaze. "How well do I know him?"

"You know, how much do you know *about* him?"

She pulled a pink blouse out of her suitcase—the one she'd been wearing when she'd met Cord—and gave it a shake. "Well, he was Michael's only brother, older by three years. He graduated with a law degree from some fancy college in the East. He's told me which one, several times in fact, but I can't seem to remember." The fact was, she didn't care.

Cord moved behind her and leaned back on the edge of the dresser. "Were Michael and Earl partners?"

He couldn't understand what a preposterous statement that was. Neither Earl nor Michael understood how to share responsibilities. They'd both been as tenacious as weeds and would have choked each other out before giving up one iota of control. She shook her head. "Earl was too much of a gambler, too aggressive in his business deals for Michael. Michael was sure and cautious. Some called it calculating."

Cord lifted a red velvet bag of potpourri she kept on her dresser and ran his thumb over the soft fabric. "What did you call it?"

Disillusionment. "My husband was a shrewd business man. If he wanted something, if he had a deal to close, nothing, and no one, could stop him."

"Were you a business deal, Rachel?"

She winced. As a love-struck young woman of twenty-two she would have never thought of her marriage as a business deal. But now...well now, she was twenty-seven and certainly not love struck. She'd realized, too late, that Michael had chosen her for her social standing and because she looked good on his arm. Drawing in a deep breath, she straightened and met Cord's intense gaze. "Yes."

His knuckles tightened around the velvet bag and the scent of roses filled the air. "He was a fool."

She turned from him then, not wanting him to see the gratitude that swelled up in her at his words. Pulling her bag of toiletries out of her suitcase, she forced a light tone to her voice. "And here, all this time, I thought that title belonged exclusively to me."

She laid the plastic bag on the bed and swerved back to the original subject. "Anyway, Earl lived a faster life than we did so we rarely saw him socially. He was away a lot of the time, traveling with the wife of the year or secretary of the week. It wasn't until after Michael died and left Earl administrator of the estate that he became so concerned with my welfare. As you heard, he thinks the ranch is a losing proposition and I should sell, put the money in something solid."

"Something like that chemical plant he mentioned tonight?"

"That's right." She suddenly realized why he'd asked her how well she knew her brother-in-law. "If you're asking me if Earl is a crook, the answer is no. He'd have no reason to steal from me. He and Michael inherited a ton of money after their parents were killed in a car accident ten years ago, then Earl inherited half of Michael's estate. The dividends from my trust fund would be paltry compared to what he makes.

"The man is simply a tightwad," she said, digging into her suitcase then gesturing widely. "He has to drink a quart of oil a day so he doesn't squeak when he walks."

When she looked back at Cord she noticed his gaze had settled on the hand she'd motioned with. Amusement slowly replaced the contemplative look in his eyes. She glanced down and realized she'd been waving a pair of silky black underwear. Quickly she tossed them into a drawer, hoping that the room was dark enough to hide the blush working its way up her neck.

"Uh, why don't you go ahead and use the bathroom while I finish unpacking?"

He took a step toward her. "In a minute."

He was too close. He smelled like the rain and lightning. She wasn't sure whether it was the storm that charged the air, or him. Either way, her skin felt alive and her breathing was labored. Apprehension, or perhaps excitement, raced up her spine. She hesitated, afraid to move lest she might reach out and touch him to see if she could feel the same electricity on his skin she felt on her own. It was quiet for a long moment, the air heavy. When he finally stepped away, she wasn't sure whether her released breath was relief or disappointment.

She watched, with surprise, as he moved around her and plopped down on the mattress.

"Great bed." He grabbed hold of the brass headboard and gave it a firm shake. It banged softly against the wall.

"Shh." Rachel held out a warning hand. "Earl's in the guest room beside us."

"Really?" With an exaggerated bounce, Cord pulled off one of his boots and it landed on the carpeting with a dull thud. "So?"

He was enjoying this, Rachel realized with annoyance. "So I'd rather not disturb him," she said through gritted teeth.

The second boot dropped to the floor. "Lord, that feels good," he said loudly, to Rachel's dismay. The headboard rocked against the wall as he continued to bounce.

Rachel bit her lip and glanced at the wall. "Cord, please, stop," she whispered. The mischievous look in his eyes and his silly bouncing almost made her smile.

"I won't stop, honey. Don't you worry about that."
He grinned at her, daring her to make him stop.

"*Cord,*" she stressed in a loud whisper, then put a
finger to her mouth. "Please!"

"I was born to please, darlin'." He grabbed hold of
the headboard and gave it an extra rattle.

A six-foot-three cowboy bouncing on the bed like a
little boy at bedtime was just too ridiculous not to
laugh at. She tried to smother her giggle behind her
hand, then forced the most serious tone she could
muster. "Cord, stop it!"

She placed a hand on his shoulder to still him, but
she might as well be trying to stop the rain. She re-
sorted to both hands on his shoulders, to no avail. He
continued to bounce and the headboard continued to
rattle.

"Sugar, I sure do like your enthusiasm," Cord said
to the wall.

Exasperated, Rachel groaned loudly, then her eyes
widened as she realized how her groan must have
sounded. "Okay, Cantrell." She grabbed the closest
weapon to her, a pillow, and hit him in the side of the
head.

As she drew back for another assault, he grabbed
her wrist and pulled her on top of him. Gasping, she
wriggled out of his hold, then smothered his face with
the pillow. She lay the full weight of her upper body
against the pillow and Cord's muffled curse made her
laugh harder.

She'd never played like this before. It was exhilarating. Arousing. She pushed that thought out of her
mind and her body and wrestled his arms down. "I've
got you now, cowboy. See how you like—"

She was on her back so suddenly, she never got the rest of her words out. Her arms were pinned at her sides and Cord's vengeful face loomed over her. "See how I like what?"

Cord watched Rachel's eyes dance with laughter. Her cheeks were flushed, her lips wide and inviting. And though he knew she was still holding back from him, it was the first time he'd really seen her smile. The first wave of desire stunned him, left him looking down at her as if he were frozen. The next wave of desire, like a blade of fire, cut deeply into him and left him aching with need.

She was so soft beneath him. So small. The kind of woman a man wanted to protect, to beat his chest over and make a fool of himself. At this moment he'd be any kind of fool she wanted. All she'd have to do was ask. He watched her eyes darken, knew that she was not unaffected by the closeness. His gaze lowered to the rapid rise and fall of her breasts. When he lowered his mouth and kissed the soft rise of her breast her quiet gasp nearly undid him.

"Oh, Rachel, what are you doing to me?" he murmured. He'd never remembered the need to be this sharp, this painful. He ran his hands up her arms, expecting her to push away from him once he released her. Instead, her hands clasped his head and she sank her fingers into his hair. She pulled him closer, moaning softly when he cupped her breasts into his palms.

Rachel thought her body was on fire. Cord's thumbs circled the hardened peaks of her nipples and she closed her eyes tightly against the sensations that rippled like liquid heat through her. She bit back a cry when he nipped gently through the thin cotton shirt she wore at the puckered tip of first one breast, then the other. She arched toward him, driven by the need that consumed her.

She heard him call her name as he lifted himself slightly and reached for the snap of her jeans. His fingers were hot against her stomach, and when the rumbling shook her, she wasn't sure if it was thunder or her own blood pounding in her temple. She opened her eyes and lightning flashed as she met Cord's fierce gaze. The look in his eyes was as wild and magnificent as the man. Rachel was suddenly, and sharply, reminded that he was not a man who built fences or laid down roots. One night with Cord, or one year. She couldn't give herself to a man who had no intention of staying.

"Cord." She laid her fingers over his. "We can't do this."

He laughed softly and pressed his lips to her temple. "Honey, unless you've got someone in your pocket, don't say 'we.' In case you hadn't noticed, I'm quite capable."

She'd more than noticed. The evidence of his arousal was pressing against her thigh right now. Blushing, she tightened her hold on his hand. "I'm sorry, Cord. I—I never meant for this to get out of control like this, but I just can't do this."

He lifted her hand in his and twisted the gold band she wore. "We *are* married, Rachel."

She lay still beneath him, trying to calm the furious pounding of her heart. "You know we're not married, not in the real sense of the word." She stared up at him. "It would be foolish to deny I'm not attracted to you, but a quick roll in the hay is not what I'm looking for. It would...complicate matters and I want us to be friends."

"Friends?" He groaned at her use of the word and rolled off her. "Good Lord, Rachel. After the way you just kissed me?" He looked at her much too smugly. "Twice in one day, as a matter of fact. You want to tell me how we're going to manage a whole year when we haven't been able to keep our hands off each other for one day?"

Her face burned in embarrassment at the truth of his sharp words. If he were angry, she couldn't blame him. She was even mad at *herself* for stopping him from making love to her. The way her body was still humming from his touch, all he'd have to do was look at her and she'd change her mind.

"We'll just have to, that's all." She rose from the bed and brushed her hair back with her fingers. "We have an agreement and I'm going to hold you to it. I can sleep on the floor tonight. After Earl's gone, you can move into the room across the hall."

Cord watched Rachel walk across the room and open an antique wooden chest. She pulled out a blanket and started to spread it on the floor. Part of him was glad that she was a lady who didn't sleep around, but the other part of him, well, the other part was damn frustrated. Frowning, he snatched a pillow and pushed himself off the bed.

"That mattress is too damn soft for me, anyway," he said gruffly, grabbing the blanket out of her hands.

"Cord, you don't have to—"

"I said I would, dammit." He tossed the blanket and pillow by the open French doors, hoping it got good and cold during the night. An icy shower was in order if it didn't.

She stared at him for a moment with doleful eyes, then turned quietly away from him to finish unpacking. Her hair, the color of warm honey, curtained her face as she bent over her task and he watched as she pushed it away from her eyes with one sweep of her slender hand. The sweet taste of her still lingered and he had to draw from the deepest resource of his will-power to prevent himself from going to her and tasting her again.

Finally she zipped up her empty suitcase and set it at the foot of the bed, then picked up a clear plastic bag filled with soaps and toothpaste and assorted female paraphernalia. Without looking at him, she made her way to the bathroom.

"Rachel."

She hesitated at the bathroom door, but did not turn around.

"I've never forced or pressured a woman to make love in my life. You can sleep easy tonight, and every night I'm in this house."

She turned to look at him then and he could see the relief and the thanks in her eyes.

"There is one thing you have to let me do though," he said, holding her uncertain gaze.

"And that is?"

"I make the coffee from now on. I doubt I'd survive a year on yours."

Laughing softly, she closed the bathroom door behind her. He pulled off his shirt, then started to pull off his jeans. He stopped, realizing it would be best if he slept with them on tonight rather than risk making Rachel any more skittish than she already was.

He lay down on the floor, punched his pillow a couple of times, then settled in, letting the sound of the rain calm his still-racing blood.

* * *

She woke leisurely the next morning, enjoying the feel of her own bed after being gone several days. Cool air rushed in from the open doors and she snuggled beneath her quilt, closing her eyes against the bright sun.

Bright sun! She sat abruptly. Good grief. How late was it? Reaching for the alarm clock by her bed, she turned it toward her, then groaned when she saw the time. Seven o'clock. She'd overslept by an hour. When she'd laid her head down on her pillow last night and focused on Cord's heavy breathing, she'd been sure she wouldn't sleep a wink. That was the last thought she remembered.

Casting a glance to the still-open French doors, she saw that Cord's blanket was folded neatly there with the pillow on top. The only thing good about over-sleeping, she decided as she jumped out of bed and dressed in record time, was that Earl would have left already and she wouldn't have to speak with him this morning.

Still, she checked out the front window on her way outside and breathed a sigh of relief to see Earl's car gone. She'd have to call him later to try and pin him down for an appointment to discuss her trust, but for now she had horses to groom and stalls to muck before it got too hot.

She was pulling her hair back into a ponytail as she made her way through the kitchen to the back door. The smell of coffee stopped her and she smiled when she saw the half-full pot. Cord Cantrell was definitely a man of his word.

She filled a cup for herself and headed for the stables. In the distance, under the shade of several oak trees, Rachel noticed Parker, her youngest ranch hand, exercising one of Cord's horses. She started to wave to him, when the sound of a diesel engine caught her ear. She stopped, then shaded her eyes as she looked to her far right, beyond the corral to the cattle pens.

Why in the world was there a cattle truck, full of cattle, on her property?

It must be some sort of mistake, she told herself as she hurried over. She better straighten this out before they unloaded. As she came around the corner of the truck a man flipped open the side gate and gave a loud "Yah!" She watched in horror as cattle streamed out of the truck and down the cattle shoot into the pens. Sam and his sons, Dave and Clint, stood by watching as the cows kept coming.

"Sam!" She called to her foreman, but his back was to her and he couldn't hear her over the bawling of the cows. That's when she saw Cord standing by the front of the truck talking with the driver.

"Cord!" She yelled his name and he looked up. He smiled and waved, then went back to his conversation. Irritated, she stalked over to him.

"What are these?" She gestured to the cattle with her cup and coffee sloshed over the sides.

"Cows, honey." He accepted the clipboard the other man handed him and signed it.

She pressed her lips together. "I know *what* they are. I want to know what they're doing here."

"I ordered them two days ago." He handed the clipboard back to the driver, then took the coffee cup from her and sipped at it.

"Cord." She took him by the sleeve and pulled him aside. The driver gave her a strange look, then climbed back into the cab of the truck. "Cord, I can't afford cattle. I thought you understood—"

"We're not buying them, we're leasing them." The truck gate slammed closed with an empty echo and the driver's helper climbed into the cab.

Her fingers tightened on his shirtsleeve. She looked over her shoulder, ready to flag down the truck before it pulled away. "What are you talking about, leasing them? Why would anyone lease a cow?"

Cord laughed. "We're not going to eat them, Rachel. We're going to use them for cutting."

"Cutting?"

"Cutting." He took another long sip of coffee, then set the cup on a bale of hay beside the corral. "That's what I do. I train and ride cutting horses." He looked at her strangely. "Didn't you realize that?"

"No." She looked at all the cows, probably three or four dozen, and wondered how she was going to pay to lease them. "I thought a horse trainer was a horse trainer. Sam always did the hiring around here."

"Relax." He took her by the shoulders and turned her to face him. "These cows will pay for themselves. All we have to do is build up a clientele."

She shrugged out of his hold. "That's easy for you to say. It takes time to build up a clientele. In the meantime, where will I come up with the money for the lease?"

Cord's jaw tightened at her use of the singular. "The cow man's a friend of mine. He knows I'm good for it. All we have to do is see that this herd gains weight before the next batch comes in. You've got plenty of pasture to make sure that happens." He put his hands on his hips. "Look, I know I should have mentioned this to you, but—"

"You're damn right you should have." She put her hands on her hips, as well.

His eyes narrowed. "And I would have, if your buddy Earl hadn't been slithering around since we arrived. I sort of had my mind on other things yesterday and last night."

His mention of the previous night made her cheeks burn, but she refused to let him throw her off track. They stared at each other for a long moment before he let out a sigh and tipped his hat back. "There's good money in cutting horses, Rachel. You're just going to have to trust me on this. And when the Fort Worth Futurity comes up in December, we'll—"

"Futurity?"

"The three-year-old competition. It's sort of like a coming-out ball for cutting horses. I entered Montana last year, and this year I'll enter Lady." Cord looked up when Sam called to him. "I'll explain in detail later. I promised the boys here I'd show them what Montana can do. If you're interested, why don't you stick around awhile and watch?"

He caught her off balance with a quick kiss on the lips, then headed for the corral. She watched Parker dismount from Montana, then hold the reins out to Cord. *If she were interested?* She wouldn't miss this for the world.

The cattle was skittish, she noticed as she threw a booted leg over the top rail of the pen and settled in to watch. Cord mounted his horse in one smooth movement, then swung the gelding around and loped into the pen.

He faced the agitated cows, lumped together in the corner farthest away, and watched them for a moment before he moved slowly forward, picking his way through the bunch of them until two or three broke off. With a command Rachel couldn't even detect, Cord swung Montana around on the largest cow of the group.

Unhappy with being separated from the herd, the cow bolted.

So did Montana, blocking the cow's escape.

It was like nothing Rachel had ever seen. If the cow so much as shifted a muscle, so did the horse. It was like a dance, a game of tag. Horse and rider were one as they hunkered down in front of the cow, purpose and determination fixed in their eyes. Cord held the reins low over the horse's neck, while his other hand gripped the saddle horn.

Rachel's heart pounded when the cow broke fast and sharp to the left. The horse followed, running to keep up, then dug its front hooves in and changed direction again when the cow did, all in a split second. Cord flowed with the horse like mercury, never missing a beat. Startled, the cow froze, unsure which way to move. Montana froze, as well, his powerful muscles tensed and ready.

Cord made it look so easy, she thought as she watched him control the horse. This was his domain; he was in complete command. The thought was unsettling, yet somehow exciting at the same time. She hadn't even realized she'd been holding her breath until he finally pulled Montana off the cow and, amidst cheers and yells from Sam and the others, rode up to her, his grin as wide as a country mile.

"So what do you think?"

She was too in awe to be casual. "I think it's the most beautiful, incredible thing I've ever seen," she said, still a little breathless.

If it were possible, Cord's grin broadened. He slid off his horse and reached out a hand to her. "Come on." He took her by the arm and lifted her off the fence. "It's your turn."

Her turn?

"What are you talking about?" She pushed away from him when he set her down next to the horse.

"You should at least give it a try, Rachel. After all, it's your ranch and you should experience firsthand what's going on."

She gasped as he grabbed her by the hips and boosted her up into the saddle. Quickly he adjusted the stirrups for her, ignoring her protests. Sam and his sons shouted encouragement from the other side of the corral.

"Cord, I can't do this." She pulled one boot out of the stirrup. "I'll fall flat on my butt."

He shoved her foot back into the stirrup. "You know how to ride, don't you?"

"Of course I know how to ride, but—"

He pulled Montana around and handed Rachel the reins. "Then just hold on tight, darlin', and go cut yourself a cow."

The horse sprinted forward when Cord clucked his tongue and Rachel grabbed the saddle horn. Heart pounding, she inched her way into the nervous herd, praying she wasn't about to make a fool—or mincemeat—out of herself. Four cows broke away to her left.

"Go get the little brown heifer, Ms. Cantrell," Sam shouted at her.

Instinctively, she pressed her right knee to the horse and they turned left, then darted forward at the touch of her boot, cutting off the brown cow from the rest of the herd. Upset, the cow bawled.

"Atta girl," Cord rooted. Sam and the rest of the men cheered.

She'd just cut her first cow.

Adrenaline pumped through her in the split second the horse and cow faced each other. Now that she had this cow, what in the world was she supposed to do with it?

Montana made the decision for her. In less than a blink of an eye, as the cow made a sharp jump left, the horse lowered its head and dipped sideways. It felt as if the horse were dropping out from under her, like the first plunge of a roller coaster after a steep climb. Rachel cried out and grasped the saddle horn tightly. They jerked to the left, then the right, moving with the upset cow.

"You're on 'im now, darlin'," Cord hollered. "Don't lose 'im!"

She heard a loud whoop and the men calling to her, but she kept her eyes on the cow, anticipating the next move, ready to go with it. It was exhilarating. Blood pounding. Montana lunged beneath her, but Rachel did not shift quickly enough with the horse. The cow dodged them and made a beeline back to the herd, jumping over his comrades in his haste.

Laughing, she swung the horse around and cantered back to Cord. His eyes were full of praise, his smile enthusiastic. "And here you told me you couldn't do it." He shook his head. "How long you been hustling cowboys?"

"I think we both know who's been hustled here, Cord." Smiling, she slid off the horse. "You knew once I got on that horse and cut that cow I'd be hooked, didn't you?''

He grinned back at her. "So do the cows stay?''

"On one condition.'' She handed the reins back to him.

"What's that?''

"That you teach me how to do that.''

Six

———

"**M**rs. Cantrell, I appreciate your enthusiasm to do business with Sweetwater First Trust and Loan, but as I've already explained to you on your last visit here— I believe it was a month ago—money is extremely tight in the market right now. I'm afraid we simply won't be able to grant you a loan."

The bank manager, a thin man with an oversize suit and graying temples, slid Rachel's application across his desk toward her. She wished she'd had time to change into something more businesslike than jeans and boots before coming to town, but there'd been work to do this morning. Plus she hadn't wanted Cord to think the trip was anything other than a supply run. It was embarrassing to be begging for money and she'd rather he didn't know.

"Mr. Raskin—" Rachel smiled politely and slid the application back again "—if you'd just look at the figures here, I'm sure you'll be encouraged by the change. In the last two weeks alone—"

"Since you married?"

She gritted her teeth. "Yes. Since I married, the Circle T has acquired eight new horses to board and train, and six new clients for lessons. With that kind of growth I'm going to need some capital for additional feed and help, not to mention repairs on the stable and fencing."

Mr. Raskin shook his head. "Economic indicators point to a downward trend for the next few months, Mrs. Cantrell. What few loans we will be granting will be based on current assets and credit history, not speculations of a profitable future. Your liabilities at this point are extremely high."

The pompous jerk. He hadn't even bothered to look at the application. Rachel widened her smile. "Mr. Raskin, once I have control of the trust fund my husband left to me, I'll be more than able to cover my liabilities, as well as repay this loan."

He nodded. "Ah, yes, the trust fund. I did speak to your brother-in-law, Earl Stephens, regarding that. He informed me those funds will be tied up for an indefinite period of time."

Damn Earl! Rachel clenched the wooden arm of the chair she sat in. He hadn't returned one of her phone calls since his visit and his secretary said he was out of town for a few days. "Those funds are no longer Mr. Stephens's concern, sir. I have authority now."

His brows rose skeptically. "I'll be happy to set up an account for you if you wish to make a transfer."

The arrogant buffoon knew she couldn't do that. Her jaw ached from the smile she'd been holding in place. "A minor legal technicality prevents me from doing that right now, but I'm sure I'll have it straightened out in a few days."

"Splendid." He folded his long, smooth fingers. "I'll just hold on to this application until then. I look forward to servicing your account."

And I look forward to taking my business elsewhere, you condescending bastard. Rising, Rachel forced herself to shake the man's clammy hand. That Michael didn't trust her to handle her own finances had been a hard enough blow, then Earl, and now Raskin. How long would it be, how many of these egotistical men was she going to have to go through before she could get control of her own life?

She'd get the money. She didn't know how, but she would. In the meantime, she'd have to keep her creditors at bay and hope like hell for a miracle.

Outside the bank, Rachel checked her watch. She'd left Cord at the barbershop when they'd gotten into town and they'd agreed to meet for lunch at the town diner. She still had twenty minutes.

Good, she thought, heading for Stockton's Feed and Grain. She had one more mission she didn't want Cord to know about. If she hurried, she had just enough time to take care of it.

"Now my oldest boy, Joe, he ain't scared to get his hands dirty like some of these kids I see today. Joe's the town mechanic, by the way, if you need any work done."

Eyes squinted, the barber—Leon was his name—stared at Cord's reflection in the mirror and asked, "You ever consider a mustache?"

Cord stared at the glob of shaving cream on his lip then glanced down at the straight razor poised there.

Deciding it best not to move his mouth at the moment, he simply grunted a negative. Shrugging, Leon swiped the cream off with two flicks of his wrist then wiped Cord's face clean with a hot towel.

"You can tell Rachel that Joe's still holding the part she ordered for her tractor, and the carburetor for her truck. Anytime she's ready, he can fix them for her."

As if the woman would listen to him. Cord had offered to have them fixed for her but she'd steadfastly refused. "I'll tell her."

Leon unsnapped the apron around Cord's neck and gave it a shake. "So you're from Montana. I got a brother in Missoula. Ever been there?"

Cord didn't remember mentioning where he was from. But then, he remembered, Sam had been in town a couple of days before. Smiling, Cord ran a hand over his hair, deciding he liked the shorter cut. "Once or twice," he answered, settling his hat over his head.

"Beautiful town, Missoula, but too much snow." The cash register bell dinged as Leon rang up the bill. "That'll be ten dollars."

After Cord paid him, Leon shoved a bowl of hard candy at him. Cord thanked him and popped a butterscotch in his mouth. "Take one of those red ones for Rachel. I always make sure I have plenty when she comes in for a trim."

"Thanks." He dropped the candy in his front shirt pocket and glanced at the wall clock. He still had twenty minutes before he met Rachel. She'd told him she had some shopping to do and from the way she'd said it, he'd assumed it was for something personal, so he hadn't pressed the issue.

These past two weeks she'd gone out of her way to avoid him. She went to bed before him and somehow managed to miss him in the morning. The only time he had her to himself was when he was giving her a cutting lesson. Either early in the morning, before his first client, or late at night, after his last, she'd show up, anxious to ride.

He hated to admit how much he looked forward to her lessons. It seemed silly to him, since he was her husband, that he valued those few minutes alone with her. She was a fast learner. Determined, tenacious. She had that same glow in her eyes about cutting that she had for her ranch.

And he was damned jealous of it.

Closing the barbershop door behind him, Cord stepped out onto the sidewalk, wondering what it would be like to have Rachel look at him like that, with her eyes all warm and eager. He wanted to know what it would feel like for her to come to him willingly, to slip into his arms and breathe that passion into him he'd already tasted and now hungered for again.

That's when he saw her, hurrying down the sidewalk several stores away. He stepped back and watched her, taking a moment to admire her long legs and rounded bottom in tight jeans. He drew in a sharp breath and shook his head. What that woman did to his male hormones was a downright sin. She stopped at the entrance to the feed store, looked around, then ducked inside.

No reason they couldn't go to lunch early, he thought, stepping back onto the sidewalk. Especially if she was done with whatever it was she'd had to do.

He ran a hand over his smooth chin and set off after her.

High clouds dotted the blue sky. It was hot today, too hot to be working the horses, so it wouldn't matter if they took a long lunch. Maybe they could even walk through town a bit, or take a drive. Better yet, they could take lunch out. He'd spotted a lake not far off the highway; it looked like a nice place to spread out a blanket. The thought of being alone with Rachel made him lengthen his stride.

They could just pick up some sandwiches, he decided as he stepped into the feed store. Maybe get a box of chocolate cookies or—

He stopped cold when he saw her.

She was standing behind the counter, with her hand resting intimately on the arm of a tall fellow who had shoulders like a bull. She was smiling and her gaze was directed coyly downward.

He stared at her, feeling as if he'd been bucked off a wild horse. The reasonable side of him told him that it probably wasn't what it looked like, that it was just an innocent encounter. But then Rachel glanced up and saw him. Her face registered guilt a yard long.

Cord told the reasonable side to go to hell.

Fists clenched, he walked stiffly over to her. "Rachel."

Cord's eyes were on the other man, who appeared startled, then embarrassed. He stepped away from Rachel and cleared his throat.

Rachel's eyes cooled as she stared at Cord. "Cord, this is Rick Stockton, a friend of mine. Rick, my husband, Cord." Rick simply nodded. He was obviously smart enough to realize that unless he wanted to lose it, he better not stick his hand out.

"I didn't realize it was already time for lunch," Rachel said, forcing a light tone to her voice.

"Obviously." Cord was trying his damnedest to control the rage he was feeling, but he didn't know how. This *thing* that was eating at him, this...jealousy...was something new to him. He felt out of control. It was like a living thing inside him, a vicious, caged-up animal that needed to be let out.

But what claim did he truly have on Rachel? he asked himself. This damn *situation* had ended up being more than he'd bargained for. A beautiful, desirable wife he could look at, but not touch. Hell, she was as skittish as a new colt whenever he even walked into the room, and here she was with this guy, as cozy as a homemade quilt. There wasn't enough land in all of Texas she could offer him to make him stomach watching her touch another man while she carried his name.

"Thanks for taking care of that for me, Rick." Rachel bent down and picked up a small, brown paper bag behind the counter. "I'll settle up with you later."

"How 'bout we settle up now?" Cord took a step forward and Rachel came around the counter, blocking his way.

"It's, ah, not necessary." Rick held up his hands and smiled nervously.

"Let's go, Cord." Her shoulders stiff, Rachel brushed past him and walked out of the store.

Deciding that Rick wasn't going anywhere for the moment, Cord turned and followed Rachel. But not before throwing the other man a look that promised pain if there was reason.

She was halfway to the diner by the time he caught up with her. He grabbed her arm and whirled her around.

"What exactly was that all about?"

Her eyes narrowed as she gripped the bag to her. "What?"

He'd never thought her the type to lie. It ate at his gut that he might be wrong. "Be straight with me, Rachel. I just caught you playing footsie with some guy and I want to know what's going on."

"Nothing was going on."

Cord wanted to punch something. Instead, he gripped both her arms and pulled her off the sidewalk out of sight. "Your face said different when I walked in on you two," he said tightly.

"I told you," she repeated carefully, "it was nothing."

Cord should have paid attention to the intensity of Rachel's words. He was just too damn mad and he couldn't stop. "If you needed a husband, then tell me how come you didn't marry Hercules in there?" He released her arms and she fell back a step. "Oh, yeah, that's right. He's not a horse trainer. You get more for your money with me."

He regretted his words the minute they came out. The look in Rachel's eyes, the bottomless hurt, knocked the edge off his anger. He clamped his mouth shut and waited for her to say something. She stared at him for a long moment and he could tell she was drawing from an inner strength that ran as deep in her as it did wide. Composed once again, she thrust the paper bag at him.

"Open it," she said with deadly quiet.

"What—"

"Open it!"

Already feeling a little foolish, he opened the bag. Inside was a box about the size of his hand wrapped in blue paper and decorated with a white bow. He had the most horrible sinking feeling as he lifted it out.

"Happy birthday, you jackass." With that, she turned and walked away.

Cord considered the date and realized it *was* his birthday. He'd never really celebrated it before, and it had been years since he'd gotten a present. But how did Rachel know? He tugged at the ribbon, peeled the paper away and lifted the lid off the box. Inside, wrapped in white tissue, was a silver belt buckle embossed with the figure of a cutting horse in action. He rubbed his thumb across the shiny surface. It felt smooth and cool beneath his touch. A tightness, like a fist, coiled around his chest.

His head snapped up. Rachel. God, what was he going to say to her?

When he found her at the diner, waiting for him in a booth, he slid next to her and took her hand.

"Since 'I'm sorry' won't quite do here—" he tightened his hold when she tried to jerk away "—how 'bout we go get the truck and you drive over me a few times?"

She said nothing, just stared icily ahead.

"Okay, you drive over me, then tie me to the bumper and drag me home."

That brought forth a half smile.

"Okay, so you drive over me, tie me to the bumper then drag me home—naked." He reached into his pocket and pulled out the candy. "Peace offering?"

She glared at him, then snatched the candy and popped it into her mouth. Cord could smell the hot cinnamon.

"You're a jerk, Cantrell. Rick is a friend of mine, that's all. If he had been any more than that you can bet I would have married him."

He wondered briefly if the man had asked her, but decided that line of thinking would only get him in trouble.

"I know. You're right, and I'm sorry."

Her chin lifted a notch and she looked away from him. He rubbed his thumb over hers, amazed she could be so soft considering how hard she worked.

"How did you know it was my birthday?"

She shrugged. "The day we met, you told me you had one coming up. I made a point to look at the marriage license when we filled it out."

Her admission made him feel strangely warm inside. He brought her hand to his lips. "I love the present."

Rachel looked down at her hand entwined with Cord's and felt her pulse speed up at his touch. Since that night he'd kissed her, she'd done her best to avoid being alone with him. All it took was the slightest touch from him, or even a look, and she could feel her resolve weakening.

Now, with his lips pressed to her wrist, she felt that same warning bell go off. He smelled like butterscotch and shaving cream and she had the most incredible urge to reach over and run her fingers over his smooth chin.

Instead, she pulled her hand out of his. "I . . . had Rick order it for me out of a catalog." Her skin still burned where he'd touched her and she resisted rubbing the sensation away. "He, uh, wrapped it for me, too."

As if in pain, Cord closed his eyes, then opened them again and rose. "Excuse me a minute, will you?"

"Where are you going?"

"Sometimes apologies don't keep, darlin'." He straightened his hat. "When the waitress gets here, just order me a crow burger."

"Hips down, Rachel! You've got to suck in your belly and squeeze your butt tight. There you go, that's it."

Rachel sat down firmly in the saddle, forcing herself to listen to Cord's instructions. She and Montana were heads down on a cow, hooves dug in.

"Don't let up," Parker shouted encouragingly from the fence rail where he'd been watching the evening's lesson.

The cow broke left.

"Stay on 'im, stay on 'im," Cord hollered. "Keep your reining hand low and your heels down. Use your calves."

An unexpected swing to the right and the cow got away. Rachel muttered a curse under her breath as she turned her horse around and faced Cord. He was grinning at her from astride a chestnut mare.

"You're not concentrating."

She shook her head as she swung down from the saddle and pulled off her gloves. That was the third cow to get away from her in five minutes. "It's just not there tonight."

They'd been working under the lights for about twenty minutes. The sky was clear, there was a whisper of a cool breeze and the air held the scent of dust mixed with anise weed.

Cord dismounted and walked over to her. "Something wrong?"

Nothing that money can't fix. She turned away from him and stroked Montana's powerful hind quarters. "No."

"You want me to take care of the horses for you, Cord?" Parker climbed down from his perch on the fence and hurried over. Cord glanced over at him. "I'd appreciate that."

"Thanks, Park." Rachel smiled at the young ranch hand as he gathered up the horses' reins. She knew he'd been working with Cord training the horses and had a bad case of hero worship. Not that she could blame him. She had one herself. In the six weeks that Cord had been here, he'd worked miracles. The ranch had better hay and feed, the bedding was top quality and there were almost enough horses boarded to pay the rent and salaries.

Too bad *almost* wasn't enough.

"What's wrong, Rachel?"

"I'm just a little tired tonight." He was blocking her way and she moved to go around him. "I think I'll just go on up to the house and—"

He sidestepped and stopped her retreat. "How come I don't believe you?"

Frowning, she pushed her hair back from her eyes. "I told you, I'm a little tired."

"If you say so," he said tightly and stepped out of her way. "I'll just mind my own business."

This time, it was she who grabbed his arm when he started to turn away. "Wait. I—I'm sorry. You're right, there is something wrong." She closed her eyes and sighed. "There's a reassessment tax due in thirty days and I can't possibly come up with the money."

"How much?" Cord asked, then whistled when she told him.

"The penalties and interest will only be more if I don't pay it. I'll get so far behind I'll never be able to catch up before I can get control of my trust."

Cord frowned at her. "I told you, I'll hire a lawyer and we'll fight the son of a—"

She shook her head. "No. I'm not using your money to fight my battles, Cord. Earl can't avoid me forever, and in the meantime, I'll manage."

Sometimes the woman was just too damn independent for her own good. Earl was conveniently hiding behind a mountain of legal red tape and there was no way to get at him or force him to relinquish power.

Yet.

In the meantime, there might be another way. "There's a futurity in three weeks in Amarillo."

Good grief, Rachel thought, here she was telling the man she was about to lose her ranch and all he could think about was a horse show. "Terrific." She clenched her hands into fists and started to walk away. "Have a great time."

"Rachel," he said behind her, "the purse is ten thousand dollars."

She stopped and whirled. "What?"

"Ten big ones." He grinned at her.

That would pay the assessment and leave enough to repair the barn roof. No. She couldn't. "That's your money if you win, Cord, not mine."

"If I win, it would be the ranch's money," he insisted.

She shook her head. "No."

Muttering an oath, Cord swung away. He put his hands on his hips and turned back. "Okay, so we'll enter you, too. The purse for nonpro is five thousand."

She would have laughed, but the only explanation for his suggestion was brain damage and she didn't want to be rude. "Cord, I appreciate the vote of confidence, but in case you weren't watching tonight, I'll clue you in. I stink."

"Winning's a mind-set, darlin'. Not only for the horse, but the rider. Your technique is fine. We're just going to have to work on that attitude of yours."

She tucked her fists at her waist and lifted her chin. "And what's wrong with my attitude?"

He laughed and moved around her, blocking her exit from the corral. "You think like a person."

The man had lost it completely, she decided as she turned to face him. "And just what am I supposed to think like?"

"A horse and a cow."

Arms outstretched, he crouched down in front of her. He had a devilish glint in his eyes.

Folding her arms, she eyed him suspiciously. "What are you doing, Cantrell?"

"Why—" he hunkered down a little lower "—I'm a cow."

She couldn't stop the laugh this time. "And I'm the horse?"

He nodded. "And a right pretty filly, too."

"This is ridiculous." She shook her head and started to walk away. He jumped in front of her.

"See if you can hold on to me, darlin'. It's worth five thousand dollars."

She rolled the figure over in her mind, then glanced around the yard to see if anyone was watching. Sam and his family had gone into town and Parker was busy with the horses. She looked at Cord, squared off in front of her, daring her. What harm would it do to humor the man?

Boots spread, she crouched and met him, face-to-face.

His smile was cocky and sure. "When you're on that horse, you've got to feel it, move with it." He shifted his weight. "Three animals, one mind."

This is pointless, she thought, but her heart started to pound and her palms were suddenly damp.

His voice lowered. "Anticipate, Rachel. What am I going to do?"

She focused on his face, watching him. He jumped to the left and so did she. Dust swirled around their legs.

"That's right." His smile widened. "Stay on me now. Don't let up."

Her body tensed and she moved with him. Left. Right. He was only inches away from her. His eyes, dark as a stormy sea, shone with excitement. She felt that excitement pump through her.

He feigned a shift left, then broke sharp right. Like a kite at the end of a string, she moved with him, blocking his exit.

Cord watched Rachel, poised and frozen in place, waiting for him to make a move. Her hair whipped around her flushed face; her eyes were narrowed and ardent, radiating passion and determination, a mixture that made his blood race and pound in his head.

He'd managed to keep his distance from her these past few weeks, since that day in town. It was for the best, he knew, but that did little to ease the ache of frustration building in him. She was driving him crazy. Just watching her muck out a stall yesterday had brought forth an erotic daydream, and the night dreams...Lord, those were enough to make him break into a sweat.

"Give up?" she taunted him, her eyes gleaming with mischief.

He smiled slowly and shifted his weight to his left.

Then he reached out and threw both arms around her.

Startled, Rachel let out a choked scream, then gasped as he lifted her off the ground. "Cord!"

"Always expect the unexpected, darlin'," Cord drawled smugly.

"That's no fair." She squirmed in protest. "Put me down."

"See what I mean?" He held her suspended. "You think like a person. Cows don't think fair. You have to think win."

"Okay, okay," she conceded, laughing. "You made your point. Now put me down."

He lowered her slowly, but did not release her. Her arms were trapped inside his. He stared down at her, watched her smile fade and her eyes meet his. The faint smell of roses drifted off her skin and he drew in the scent.

He had to taste her. Just once more. Expecting her to fight him, he tightened his hold on her and lowered his mouth before she could protest. He watched as her head fell back and her eyes drifted closed.

Rachel could have sworn her bones were melting. Cord's breath fanned her cheek as his lips brushed over hers. She tried to remember why she'd been fighting this for so long, but she couldn't think. And even if she could, it wouldn't matter. She whispered his name and marveled at the longing she heard in her own voice. He kissed the corners of her mouth and his tongue skimmed her bottom lip. Desire shot though her like an arrow of fire. She needed to touch him, draw him closer to her, but she couldn't, not with her arms trapped. She struggled to free them.

"Don't fight me, Rachel." Cord's voice was ragged. "Please, just let me kiss you."

Fight him? Good God, couldn't the man see, couldn't he feel, what was happening? She started to pull away, to tell him.

"Hey, Cord—". Parker's shout made Rachel freeze "—I put Montana on the hot walker and—oops."

Parker stopped in his tracks at the sight of Rachel in Cord's arms and, red-faced, whirled around with a mumble of apology.

His jaw clenched tight, Cord released Rachel. She stumbled backward, amazed that her knees were able to hold her up.

"I'm sorry," he said tightly, drawing in a deep breath. "I told you I'd never force you. I—I guess I just lost it there for a moment."

Sorry? He'd just kissed her with enough heat to melt glass and he was *sorry?* She felt her cheeks burn and she quickly hid her embarrassment behind a casual toss of her head. "What was it you said, 'Always expect the unexpected'? I'd say you demonstrated your point rather well."

"Dammit, Rachel, I didn't kiss you to prove a point."

"Forget it," she said flatly, knowing she never would. "It was just a kiss."

His eyes narrowed. "Right."

She forced herself to think about business, about the ranch. "What I want to know is," she said, pushing the hair out of her eyes with still shaky fingers, "do you really think we can win that competition?"

Her sudden change of subject seemed to surprise him. He nodded slowly.

She raised her eyes to his and smiled. "So where do we sign up?"

Seven

"And that was Mark Holden riding Little Leroy for the Tully M Ranch, folks, and a fine job it was," the announcer called out. *"With a final score of 222 in the Abilene nonpro open, that young man and little colt will be a hard team to beat."*

The crowd cheered and applauded as the rider tipped his hat and walked his horse out of the arena. The announcer then signaled the next rider into the pen.

Rachel sat back in the saddle, closed her eyes, then drew in a deep breath.

She was the final entrant, after the next rider.

"You okay?"

She let her breath out slowly and opened her eyes. Cord was staring up at her with concern. His hand rested on her thigh and even through the soft leather of her chaps and jeans his touch calmed her. "About the same as I was yesterday, and the day before that."

"Good." He squeezed her leg. The belt buckle she'd given him shone brightly at his waist. "Those two days are what got you into the finals, darlin'. Just keep doing whatever it is you've been doing."

"There's nothing left to do any more of that." She pressed a hand to her stomach and grimaced. She'd just lost her breakfast in the bathroom, as she had every other day, before every ride.

He chuckled softly. "Then there's nothing to worry about. All you have to do is get out there and show everyone what your horse can do."

She still couldn't believe she'd come this far. When they'd checked into a suite at the hotel two days ago, she'd never expected to get past the first go-round. She turned at the sound of excited whoops from the crowd and watched a contestant's horse drop down beautifully on a calf. Her stomach felt like an electric blender turned on high.

"Easy for you to say, Cantrell." She turned back and tugged the brim of her white hat snugly in place. "You got to the finals in the open division as smooth as silk."

Cord checked her stirrups and made sure they were even. "I haven't won yet, Rachel, and you haven't lost."

"Cord." She shook her head. "How am I ever going to beat a 222?"

"With a 223." His hand closed over hers. "What did I teach you?"

There was strength in his hand. Comfort. She sat up straight. "Winning's an attitude."

He smiled. "That's my girl. Now go get yourself a calf."

The buzzer sounded, signaling the end of the current rider. His score was 223.

Her insides felt as if they'd dropped down to her knees. Sucking in a deep breath, she swung her horse around and entered the arena.

"Come on, Montana," she whispered. "Let's pick one out and show those judges just what you can do."

For the next two and a half minutes, Rachel let instinct guide her. When the buzzer sounded, the announcer complimented her, then paused as he waited for her score: 223½.

The crowd cheered. Somewhere, a horn blew. Stunned, Rachel raised her hat.

She'd won. *She'd won.*

She was barely through the arena's gate when a pair of strong hands gripped her waist and pulled her out of the saddle. "Cord!" He lifted her off the ground and swung her, then smothered her laugh beneath his lips. She wrapped her arms around his neck to steady herself. Excitement poured through her, whether from the win or his kiss, she wasn't sure, but she tightened her hold on him. White-hot desire shot through her and she pressed closer, deepening the kiss.

Suddenly, they were torn apart by well-wishers. Cord was congratulated on his training skills, Rachel for her riding. The attention was heady, but she'd never wished more in her life that she could be alone. With Cord. Their eyes met for a brief, intense moment before Rachel was pulled in a dozen directions. Her picture was snapped as she hugged Montana, and a professional video man recorded the brouhaha while a reporter conducted a brief interview first with her, then with Cord.

She'd had diamonds and fast cars and attended some of the most glamorous parties in the world. But nothing, *nothing* came close to the thrill of winning her first competition. She'd never felt so happy or content. She laughed when Cord winked at her while he was talking to another trainer. It just couldn't get any better, she thought.

But when Cord won the pro open, it did.

The excitement of the day stretched into the evening when the hotel hosting the horse show put on a barbecue to celebrate closing day. Paper lanterns dotted the lawns and walkways; strings of miniature lights sparkled in the trees and the smell of sizzling steaks and chicken wafted on the cool night air. Beneath the clear ceiling of a million stars, a live band played country-western music loud and fast. Rachel had finally discovered something that cowboys did harder than ride horses.

Party.

Out of breath, she put up a hand to beg off another dance with a ranch hand from Abilene and then collapsed onto a bench beneath a low-branched oak. She'd been on a whirlwind since her win this afternoon and it was nice to have a moment alone.

Five thousand dollars.

She smiled. It wasn't as big a purse as Cord's had been, but it was enough to pay the tax at least. The barn roof would just have to wait, and so would the truck and fencing. They'd waited this long, so how much difference would another few weeks possibly make?

Her gaze scanned the crowd, looking for one special white hat that was taller than the rest. Cord had been dragged away some time ago by a group of cowboys from Pipe Creek. He looked so handsome tonight in his dress clothes that she hated to let him out of her sight. Especially after noticing the looks he'd received from the ladies at the party. She smiled to herself. He might not be her husband in the true sense of the word, but the women here didn't need to know that.

How would she ever replace him after they went their separate ways? she wondered, closing her eyes as she listened to the distant call of a nightingale. He was a great horseman, the best trainer she'd ever seen, and everyone on the Circle T would miss him.

But not nearly as much as she would.

She knew she was coming to depend on him too much, and she didn't want that. Still, knowing he was there gave her comfort and a sense of contentment she'd never felt before. And there were other feelings. Feelings she chose not to identify, or give credence to, but they picked away at her just the same. Sighing, she lifted the hair off her shoulders, letting the night air cool her heated neck.

There'd be no one to replace Cord. She knew that with her mind and her heart. But it would do her no good to think about that now.

Tonight, just this one night, what would be the harm in pretending, even to herself, that he wouldn't be leaving?

From an outside corner of the dance floor, Cord spotted Rachel sitting under the tree and made his way over to her. He'd seen her dancing with several of the men, but he hadn't been able to break away from his conversation with a trainer from Pipe Creek until just now. He knew she was still reveling in the excitement of her win today and he didn't want to cut in on that, but he'd already decided she was his the rest of the evening.

She looked beautiful tonight. Her dress was turquoise, with leather and sequins stitched around the shoulders. The waist was narrow, the skirt long and full and when she spun on the dance floor he'd been glad she wore white boots so no one else could see her long, slender legs.

Watching her now, sitting on the bench, with her eyes closed and her back arched as she lifted her hair off her neck, he nearly stopped dead in his tracks. She looked so damned tempting, all he could think of was dragging her back to the hotel room and peeling that dress off of her. He'd spread those long legs of hers and make love with her until they both collapsed.

He swallowed hard and cursed his line of thinking. He had vowed not to force the issue with her, but sharing the suite with her had been more difficult than he could have imagined. Just knowing she was on the other side of the wall was driving him crazy. He'd woken up in a sweat the past two nights, with the sheets from the pullout couch twisted under him.

He stepped in front of her now, so close he could smell the enticing scent that was hers alone. Her cheeks were pink from the dancing, her lips slightly parted as she lifted her hair off her shoulders. He clenched his hands into fists to stop himself from pulling her to him. His stomach was twisting. Dammit, they were going to have to talk about this. He wasn't made of stone. If she didn't want him, then he knew where he could go and find a woman who did.

She opened her eyes then and what he saw there held him frozen. It was the look, that same look she always had when she thought of the ranch. Only now she was looking at him with that same intensity, that same warmth and excitement.

He saw the passion there, but wondered if he imagined it because he wanted it so badly. All the frustration, the aching, it had all been worth what he saw in the depths of her eyes now. When she smiled, all rational thought left him. He was sinking in quicksand and powerless to stop it. He'd only been fooling himself to think he could go to another woman as long as there was a chance with Rachel. If he had to wait a whole damn year, hell, a lifetime, then he'd wait if it meant he could hold her and have her look at him like that again.

His pulse was racing as he reached for her hand and they walked toward the other couples on the dance floor. Tonight, he decided as he pulled her into his arms, Rachel would not be dancing with anyone else.

Rachel let herself go. Though she didn't quite understand the mood that had suddenly come over Cord, she fell under the spell of the evening. She wasn't going to think, she was going to feel.

She slid into Cord's strong arms and pressed her cheek against his white shirt. His scent was intoxicating, an earthy, masculine scent that made her suddenly understand how truly clever nature was. She was responding, at a very basic level, to something she couldn't see, or even touch. Perfume makers couldn't come close to bottling anything this potent, this powerful. It was dangerous to be so close with this man, to know that they'd be going back to their hotel room together, alone. She tried to tell herself she was only dancing like this for appearance' sake. But if that were true, then why were her insides coiling like wire and her heart pounding like a bass drum?

Cord couldn't get close enough to her. They'd probably be arrested if he tried. Their bodies moved with the music, but what they were doing was not called dancing. He ran his hands down her back, trying like hell to remind himself they were in a public place.

Her fingers rested lightly on his neck and he doubted that she realized she was caressing him there. An ache spread through him, like a bottomless pit, and he knew that even if he were to have her it would not ease. It would only grow worse and be more demanding. The thought terrified him, but still, like a crazy man, he couldn't stop himself. He brushed his lips against her temple, felt her pulse racing out of control. He knew she wanted him every bit as much as he did her.

What was the point in holding back?

"Rachel." Her eyes were closed and he kissed them.

"Hmm?"

"Let's go back to the room."

Her eyes fluttered open. They were dark with passion, filled with wonder. She started to open her mouth to speak when suddenly the band stopped playing and the drums rolled.

Two men walked up to Cord and Rachel. One was dressed like a sheriff from the Old West. The second man was his deputy. Their expressions were grim.

"Mr. and Mrs. Cantrell?" The sheriff hitched up his pants.

Gritting his teeth, Cord released Rachel and turned to the man. "Yes?"

The sheriff cleared his throat. "You're both under arrest."

Even though he knew it was all in fun, Cord felt like throttling the man. "For what?"

"Cattle rustling," he replied. "We'll have to hold you both—" he pointed to a cardboard structure painted like a jail cell "—until someone puts up bail."

Why now? Cord groaned silently, allowing the deputy to put plastic handcuffs on him. Of all the miserable, rotten timing!

Rachel cast Cord a quick glance as she was handcuffed and led away. The crowd cheered and booed. Shaking his head, Cord muttered a curse under his breath and followed.

Cord slipped the key into the hotel room door and opened it. It was after midnight, he noted sullenly. Once he and Rachel had been made the center of attention, it seemed that there was just no getting away, even after they'd been bailed out of "jail." Reluctantly, Cord had to admit that he'd had a good time, despite his frustration.

Flipping on the light, he watched Rachel as she moved past him into the room. She was humming softly, and her eyes were still lighted from the excitement of the evening. They'd be leaving in the morning, going back to the ranch, and he knew once they were there that she would slip back behind that wall she'd constructed between them.

And could he blame her? he wondered, tossing the key onto the table beside the couch. She'd had more than her share of men riding herd over her. She deserved more than that. She deserved the kind of man who'd be there for her, not for a year, but for a lifetime. He thought of his own life, all the years of drifting, the lonely nights. If there were a chance, any chance at all...

No. The fact was, cowboys made rotten husbands. Isn't that what his mother had told his father repeatedly before she finally left? Over the years, Cord had seen time and time again that it was true. Horsemen were always thinking about the next horse, the next show. It would only be a matter of time before he'd have to move on.

He wanted Rachel physically, but the idea of settling down with children and dinner bells, that scared the hell out of him more than a three-thousand-pound angry bull. The idea of a home, a real home, as Rachel had said, had never been more than a brief fantasy for him. After tonight, after seeing the way Rachel had looked at him, he knew he didn't want to hurt her any more than she'd already been hurt. If he had to take cold showers and work sixteen-hour days for the next year, then that's what he'd do, dammit.

His resolve slipped a notch when she touched his arm.

"I had a wonderful time tonight, Cord. Thank you."

When she kissed his cheek, he clenched his jaw and smiled tightly. "Me, too."

She stared at him for a moment, then smiled back. "Good night."

" 'Night."

He watched her walk—or was it more of a saunter?—into the bedroom and close the door behind her.

He wondered how far he could turn up the cold faucet.

Drawing a deep breath, he walked out onto the private patio of their sixth-floor room. All he needed was a few moments to compose himself, then he'd drink himself into a stupor. Even though he'd pay for it in the morning, it would be worth it if he could drown out the dreams for just one night.

A cool breeze drifted onto the patio, bringing with it the lonesome quiet of the city below. The soft glow of street lamps lighted the empty streets. Houses were dark. Everyone was in bed...the last place he wanted to be right now. A noise behind him caught his attention.

His heart stopped when he turned.

Rachel was standing there, dressed in an emerald-green silk robe. It was tied at the waist, but the slit up the front revealed enough leg to make his blood pound like a hammer. She glided toward him with a whiskey glass in her hand and a smile on her lips.

"I thought you might be thirsty."

He felt as if he'd swallowed a cotton sock. He reached for the glass, covering her hand with his, holding it there for a moment as he drank in the sight of her. The robe turned her eyes a deep forest green and her lips were sultry and inviting.

He took the glass and downed half the contents, thankful for the bite of the whiskey as it rolled down his throat.

"Rachel, honey," he said, his voice ragged, "if you're trying to test me, I better warn you, I'm failing something miserable. If you don't get out of here, in about two seconds that little lick of cloth is going to be six stories down and you are going to be on your back under me."

Her lips curved into a satisfied smile. She took the glass from him and downed a fair swallow. Her eyes widened, then she set the glass down on the patio table.

"Why, Cord," she said, her voice husky, "have you always been such a romantic?"

It was all he needed to hear. He reached out and with one snap of his wrist the tie was undone and the robe slid down her smooth skin. What she had on underneath set off skyrockets in his head and fire in his veins: a green teddy edged with black lace, cut high on her long slender thighs and low on her rounded breasts.

Rachel gasped when Cord pulled her against him. Though she'd seen the look in his eyes, the primitive, wild hunger, she hadn't expected it to be so strong. After she'd danced with him at the party tonight she'd known, as only a woman can, that they would make love tonight. The anticipation had only made the wait sweeter. When Cord had not come to her, well, she'd taken matters into her own hands.

And now, it seemed, he had taken matters back into *his* hands.

His hands slid over the smooth silk at her waist, then down and over her buttocks as he lifted her against him. He was already hard and fully aroused. That knowledge only intensified her own need, a need so strong that she called his name and urged him on. His arms came around her as he fitted her to him and carried her into the bedroom and laid her down on the soft mattress.

He covered her body with his and his lips claimed hers possessively, as if she might slip away from him. She wrapped her arms around him, pulling him tighter, tasting the whiskey on his tongue. He breathed fire into her, igniting her as his hands slid the thin straps off her shoulders, pulling the silk roughly out of his way. His hands were hot on her skin and she felt as if she might burst into flames as he cupped her breasts and caressed them.

He tore his mouth from hers and trailed kisses down her neck until he reached one swollen, aching nipple. She cried out, burying her hands in his hair as his tongue slid over the pearled peak of her breast. His fingers worked magic, caressing, sliding over her skin. Seconds later, the teddy was gone and she lay naked beneath him.

He only dreamed she could be this passionate, that she would want him as much as he wanted her. The feeling was exhilarating, intoxicating. He tugged at the buttons of his shirt as her fingers worked open the snap of his jeans. Her hands were smooth as she slid them down his hips and tugged the pants out of the way. Her skin was soft and delicate and he pulled back, worried he might hurt her. But she was as desperate for him as he was for her and her whispered pleas were driving him crazy. He cursed his own lack of control, but the weeks of wanting her, of dreaming about her, made the pain unbearable.

She wrapped her arms around him, and he drove deeply into her, groaning with pleasure at the slick tightness of her as she took him in. She arched and met him thrust for thrust, crying out as the need built and the fire exploded in them both. She clung to him as he shuddered and called her name again and again.

Neither one of them knew how long they lay there. It could have been seconds, or minutes. He began to move again, more slowly now, and time no longer mattered.

Cord woke gradually, on his side, with the bright sun beating on his bare shoulders. He wrapped his arms around Rachel and she snuggled closer, pressing her back against his chest. Her sigh of contentment brought a smile to his lips. He kissed her shoulder, then slowly worked his way up.

"You shouldn't do that," she said sleepily, stretching her neck so that he could.

"Why?" He moved his lips to the back of her neck, wondering if he'd imagined that sensitive spot there last night.

"Because—" she sucked in her breath when his teeth nipped her skin "—we're going to get kicked out of here pretty soon. It's almost checkout time."

This was definitely the spot, he decided when she moaned softly and arched her back. "Darlin'," he murmured, "it would take the combined forces of every Texas Ranger to get me out of this bed with you."

Rachel smiled. Her skin felt alive and tingling and with Cord kissing her neck like that she couldn't lay still. When his hand cupped her breast and his thumb circled her nipple, she bit her lip and turned her head against his shoulder.

"I don't think I'll be able to walk again," she said roughly. "Are you ever satisfied, Cantrell?"

He laughed and slid a hand over her sleek hip. "Why don't we find out?"

Rachel closed her eyes tightly and shuddered as his hand dipped down between her legs. Her body ached for his touch. She cried out when his fingers slipped slowly into her and she moved against him.

Cord fought to keep his own raging desire under control. He wanted to please Rachel, watch her in the morning sun as he loved her. Her eyes were closed, her dark, thick lashes fanning her flushed cheeks. She moaned then and moistened her lips with her tongue before catching her lower lip between her teeth. His control shattered when she moaned again. He turned her to him and entered her with the same driving force he'd felt last night. She lifted herself to meet him, her need as fierce and potent as his. The tremor started as a deep, uplifting roll, then struck with a jolt, shattering inside her like sparkling glass. A moment later, Cord shuddered with the same intense need, calling her name as he pulled her roughly to him.

When he could think again, Cord rose on his elbows and eased his weight off Rachel. Her skin glowed from their lovemaking and her eyes, dark and dreamy, focused on him through lowered lashes. He kissed her nose and smiled. "What were you saying about *me* being satisfied?"

"Don't be impertinent, cowboy." She poked one slender finger in his chest. "Just feed me. I'm starving."

Rachel watched the devil dance in Cord's eyes. When he bent down to kiss her, she wiggled out from under him and sat on the edge of the bed. It had been the most incredible night of her life. She took in the scattered clothes and rumpled bedspread lying on the floor, then swallowed hard and ran a hand through her tousled hair.

So, what now?

She glanced over her shoulder at him lying naked on the bed and she felt strangely shy. She looked away, her gaze searching the room for something to put on. Her teddy lay at her feet, next to Cord's black briefs. She felt her cheeks burn. She jumped when his hand took hold of her arm and gently tugged her back onto the bed.

"Don't, Rachel."

She avoided his gaze. "Don't what?"

He placed a finger under her chin and tilted her face up, forcing her to look into his eyes. "Don't be embarrassed about spending the night with me. It's not like that with you and me. We both waited a long time for this and we also both knew it was inevitable."

She met his intense gaze and nodded. He was right, of course. Though she'd denied it, fought it, she'd known this would happen. That she wanted it to happen. "I'm just not sure what to say now that, well, you know—" she felt her cheeks burn "—now."

"What did you think?" he said, exaggerating his drawl. "That I'd put a notch on my boots, hitch up my pants and say, 'Thank ya kindly, ma'am. That was right nice.'"

She laughed and let herself relax a little.

"Last night was special to me, Rachel." He cupped her face in his large, rough hands. "You're special to me."

He lowered his mouth to hers and kissed her so gently, she thought she might cry. Last night wasn't going to be enough, she knew. She wasn't sure there ever would be with him. Not now. Not after he'd turned her inside out and upside down. She realized at this moment what she'd been fighting all along. She'd known instinctively what would happen if she let her guard down. She'd need him. She'd depend on him.

And she'd love him.

Later, she thought, pulling him to her once again. She'd deal with that later, when they left this fantasy world and surfaced to the cold reality of life.

Eight

It was hot. Miserably, unbearably, and irritably hot. Rachel rolled up her sleeves and pulled her work gloves on, then grabbed a shovel and started on the first stall. Horses needed a fresh bed whether it was hot or not, she noted grimly.

Normally this work would be done before the sun was up so far, but today she'd overslept. She smiled, remembering the night of passion she'd shared with Cord. It had been a month since the horse show and he'd gradually moved his things into her room until it was no longer a question of where he would be sleeping.

Frowning, she wiped the sweat from her brow and dumped a load of manure into the wheelbarrow. Cord and she had . . . an understanding, though an unspoken one. No emotional ties, no promises. They worked together all day long, ate dinner, then shared a bed.

And what was wrong with that? she asked herself, dumping another load. Why not enjoy each other for the remainder of the time he'd be here and then, well, then he'd have his land, she'd have her ranch and life would go on. Hesitating, she pressed the shovel's handle to her forehead and closed her eyes.

She was as full of it as the wheelbarrow.

Rachel swallowed hard to clear the thickness in her throat, then pulled off a glove to wipe a tear away. Damn if she wasn't getting maudlin. She was a big girl. She'd known what she was getting herself into when she made love with Cord.

No, that wasn't true, she sighed. Nothing could have prepared her for the roller-coaster ride she'd been on since that night after the horse show. There was no way she would have ever believed she'd fall so deeply and so completely in love.

But she had. And she'd just have to deal with it.

Squaring her shoulders, she tugged her glove back on and forced herself to think of the positive. They had enough horses boarded to pay the mortgage and the ranch hands. The winnings from the horse show had taken care of the taxes and fixed the tractor. Now she just had to come up with enough to repair the barn roof and the fencing on the south border. Oh, yes, and the carburetor on her truck needed rebuilding. She sighed and bent back to her work. The truck would have to wait.

She was sure it would only be a short time—maybe a few more weeks—before she gained control of her money. Cord had continued to insist that he pay for a lawyer to fight Earl, but she'd refused. If she took Cord's money, it would give him that edge over her, that final straw of control, and he already had way too much. Never again would she give a man that kind of power over her.

She paused in her work to catch her breath. Damn, but this heat and humidity were oppressive. She smiled. Still the night had been worth it.

"It's too hot for you to be doing that."

She swung around at the sound of Cord's voice. He'd been getting ready to drive into town when she'd come out to the stable and she'd expected him to be gone by now.

She dumped another load and turned to face him, wondering why he looked so serious. "I wouldn't be doing this now," she said in her best femme fatale voice, "if someone hadn't kept me up all night and then let me oversleep."

One corner of his mouth twitched at her comment, then he frowned. "There was a phone call for you from a Mr. Raskin."

Rachel lowered the shovel. She had an appointment with the banker tomorrow, but she hadn't wanted Cord to know. "Thank you." She turned back to her work. "I'll call him later."

"That won't be necessary." Cord took the shovel out of her hands and laid it aside. "He's canceling his appointment with you. Said that after reviewing your application, he's afraid he'll have to deny the loan."

Damn that weasel Raskin! What business was it of his to tell Cord? Rachel met his hard gaze.

"Why didn't you tell me, Rachel?" He swung away from her. "Just once, couldn't you tell me whatever problems you're having and let me help?"

Rachel straightened. "You mean let you loan me money?"

"Yes, dammit, if that's what you need!" He swung back around, his eyes narrowed and his jaw clenched. "How do you think it makes me feel that you'll go to the bank and not me? That you won't even let me take your truck in and get it fixed, even though it breaks down on you every other day."

Cord knew he was shouting but he just didn't care. When he'd taken that phone call from Raskin, it was like a red flag. Damn this woman's independence. Enough was enough.

"I'm sorry if it makes you angry, Cord," Rachel said with dead calm. "But the ranch's expenses are mine, not yours. Our agreement—"

"Damn the agreement!"

There was a flicker of fear in her eyes, then a shutter pulled down over her face. "Are you saying you want out?"

"Oh, for God's sake, Rachel." He slammed his fists on his hips. "No, that's not what I'm saying. I just thought what we had was a little more than a damned agreement!"

Her heart skipped a beat, then raced. Carefully, she met his gaze. "Do we?"

His eyes bore into hers. "Of course we do. I care about you, about the ranch. I want to help. We're partners, remember?"

He *cared* about her. No word of love. *Partners*.

"Right. Partners." The ache in her chest made it hard to breathe. She picked the shovel up and went back to work. "But I'm still not going to borrow any money from you, Cord, so let's drop it. It's too damn hot to argue."

Blast the woman! Cord ground his back teeth together as he watched her swing the shovel, sweat dripping from her brow. The additional horses and paperwork to run the ranch were taking their toll on her. Shadowed circles rimmed the bottom of her eyes and he'd noticed she hadn't been as alert during her lessons the past couple of weeks.

She was pushing herself to the edge, refusing to listen to suggestions that she slow down. He might have moved into her bedroom, but he certainly hadn't moved into any other aspect of her life. Strange, but once he'd thought that would have been enough, sharing a bed with Rachel. It surprised him, and angered him that it wasn't enough. He wanted more, but he didn't have the right to ask for it, because he knew he couldn't offer the same in return.

Scowling, he jammed his hat lower down on his head. She looked as if she were about ready to keel over in this heat. Her blue shirt was soaked with sweat and she was flushed bright red. The woman just didn't know when to stop.

Fists clenched, he yelled over his shoulder. "Parker!" Two seconds later, the ranch hand stuck his head in the door of the stable. "Would you please muck this stall out for Mrs. Cantrell?"

When she started to protest, he turned on his heels. "I'm going to town," he snapped over his shoulder. "And I'll pick up that damn carburetor whether you like it or not."

Furious, Rachel watched Cord leave. She wasn't about to start a fight in front of Parker, but later—she narrowed her eyes—later, they'd talk about this.

"Thanks, Parker." She forced a smile and handed him the shovel. "I'm going to drive over to the south border and check on those broken fences. I'll be back in about an hour."

Climbing into her truck, Rachel slammed the door and swore fiercely when the engine cranked but wouldn't start. After several tries, the motor revved to life.

There. She lifted her chin with a satisfied nod and jammed the gear shift into drive. *This truck works just fine.*

And when Cord came back from town she'd tell him exactly what he could do with that carburetor.

An hour later, Rachel stood, hands on her hips, beside a dead truck. She shook her head, wondering if there was something she'd forgotten to do. Swearing hadn't worked, nor had sweet-talk, pumping the gas or hitting the carburetor.

She was stuck.

Damn! Biting the inside of her cheek, she glanced up at the sky and frowned. The air had become heavy, almost suffocating, and big, boiling dark clouds loomed ominously on the horizon. She'd never seen weather quite like this before and she felt a strange uneasiness creep through her.

She thought about walking back to the ranch, but if it started to rain she'd be drenched. She shrugged. Well, there was a saying in Texas she'd certainly found to be true: If you don't like the weather, wait five minutes. She glanced back at the ragged mass of ominous clouds. It would probably be best if she just stayed put. She could hole up in the cab of the truck, if necessary. At least the blasted vehicle would be good for something.

Why was it so quiet? she wondered, scanning the area. It seemed as if the land had emptied of all life.

No sound, no movement. Confused, she knelt beside the truck in the shade of the cab.

Would Cord come looking for her when he got back from town? He'd been mad when he left, but he wasn't the type who stayed mad. She closed her eyes, already imagining the smug look he'd have on his face.

But he *had* been right, she thought. That's what really irritated her. Here she was, trying to prove to him she could take care of herself, and now she would have to sit here and wait until he rescued her. Sighing, she reached down and picked up several pebbles, then tossed them, one at a time, at a blue sagebrush. Why couldn't he understand how important her independence was to her? She couldn't let up or give in. It would only make it that much more difficult when he left.

Partners. That's what he'd called them. She wasn't even sure why that had upset her. She'd needed a reminder that business was what their relationship was based on, not love.

For Cord, anyway.

For the second time today, she blinked back tears. How was she ever going to let him go?

There was a sound, a strange sound, like a freight train approaching. She glanced up and realized the air had turned a sickly yellow. Dropping the pebbles still in her hand, she rose and looked off to the horizon. A band of fear gripped her chest when she saw the funnel-shaped formation rising hideously from the pale ground to the black sky.

Tornado.

Something was wrong.

Cord pressed his foot to the accelerator and leaned

forward in his seat. He'd almost made it to town when he'd turned around and headed back to the ranch. This time, he decided, he and Rachel were going to have it out. Whatever it took to get through that thick skull of hers, then that's what he'd do. He had to make her see that driving herself the way she was would do more harm than good. Whether she liked it or not, he'd hire a lawyer to take care of Earl, or—Cord clenched his jaw —he'd take care of the bastard himself.

Damn, but the woman was headstrong. But then, weren't those fillies the ones most fun to tame? It was hard for him to imagine Rachel as tame, and that pleased him. During the day she was all business and formality and stubborn as a mule; at night she was as beautiful and free as any wild mustang.

He looked forward to the nights.

Anxious, he pushed the gas pedal harder and watched the sagebrush and devil brush pass by in a blur. Rachel worked as hard as any man, harder probably, but at night, when she came to him…Lord, but she was sweeter and softer than any woman he'd ever known. She'd made him want things he'd never thought possible. Things that terrified him.

He rubbed the back of his neck, trying to erase the uneasiness twisting up his spine and spiraling in his gut. Something was wrong. He knew it; he could feel it. But what?

He let out an impatient sigh and told himself he was overreacting. He'd had a fight with Rachel, it was hot and so damn humid he couldn't breathe. . . .

Couldn't breathe. Alert now, Cord whipped his eyes to the horizon and saw the black clouds, felt the heaviness of the air. And the color. He'd seen that color before, two years ago in Abilene.

Panic gripped him. He floored the pedal and flipped on the radio.

"*—on the tornado watch for the Sweetwater area. Residents, please be advised to seek available shelter. The twister is moving southwest about thirty miles an hour. More updates as information becomes available, but for now, these are listings of local public shelters—*"

Damn! He turned off the highway, toward the ranch, spewing dust and dirt as the back wheels spun out. The sky was blacker, more ominous now, but he saw no sign of the twister yet. Maybe it would bypass them.

He skidded to a stop in front of the stables and jerked the truck door open. Startled, Parker looked up from the trough he'd been scrubbing out.

"Where's Rachel?" Cord yelled, running into the stables.

Confused, Parker set the brush down and rubbed his hands on his jeans. "She went to check on some broken fences."

Swearing, Cord ran back out. "Where?"

Parker scratched his head. "Well, I'm not sure, maybe the south border, but—"

"Dammit, Parker—" Cord grabbed the younger man by the shirtfront "—there's a twister coming and Rachel may be in its path. Now you think hard and tell me where she went."

Parker swallowed hard. "The south border. I'm sure."

It was the sound that caught both men's attention. A deep, rolling growl. When they looked up, it was there, in the distance, a narrow, whirling funnel.

Cord released Parker. "Go tell Sam and his family to get in the shelter and stay there. I'm going after Rachel."

His face ashen, Parker nodded, then turned and ran. Cord jumped back in the truck and tore off.

In a matter of minutes the tornado would be over the south border and headed this way.

White-knuckled, Cord gripped the steering wheel and floored the accelerator.

He had to get to her before that twister did.

Rachel watched the tornado approach as if it were a giant's spinning top. Tumbleweed flew by her. The sky was deathly black; the wind roared in her ears. Her heart slammed in her chest as she stood there, mesmerized by the imposing display of nature. The twister dipped up and down, a gray whirling mass that stretched into the heavens. She took in the incredible sight, feeling as if it weren't real, but rather a horrific, spectacular dream.

But it wasn't a dream. And it was coming right at her.

For God's sake, Rachel, this is no time to sightsee. If she didn't move fast, in about two minutes she was going to find herself taking the ride of her life.

She whipped her head around, searching frantically for some kind of shelter, but she was at least a mile from the ranch on flat, open range. She glanced at the truck, but dismissed it. It wouldn't run and it sure as hell wouldn't protect her.

A tumbleweed slammed into her and she tossed it aside. Wind whipped at her hair and her clothes.

Run, dammit! But where?

She staggered backward, feeling as if her boots were filled with rocks and her legs made of sponge. A rabbit sped by her and Rachel watched as it dropped down out of sight into a ditch maybe fifty yards away.

It was like a nightmare, one where you couldn't catch your breath and your legs wouldn't move. The funnel moved closer, like a snake writhing and hopping across the land. The wind increased and the sound, like a giant blowtorch, shuddered through her. She turned and stumbled after the rabbit.

Low, she had to get low. Judging how far away the tornado was, and how fast it was moving, Rachel guessed she had less than a minute to dig herself in somewhere. She yanked herself out of the nightmare and pumped energy into her legs, running faster than she'd ever run in her life. The wind screamed at her. The sky rolled threateningly.

Headfirst, she pitched herself over the edge of the ditch and landed sharply against a boulder. Pain was like a white-hot mist in front of her eyes and she blinked it away, burrowing herself as low as possible. Rocks and brush jabbed at her face and arms.

The sound was deafening. A hideous howling that penetrated her body. Clouds of dirt and debris stung her eyes as the whirling mass passed no more than fifty yards from her. She lifted her head, letting out a cry as she watched the funnel sweep up her truck as if it were no more than a piece of cardboard, then spit it back out again, sending it crashing on its side like a broken toy.

The tornado moved on then, jumping and dancing across the range, leaving the landscape wiped clean wherever it touched down. As she watched it retreat and move toward the ranch she thought of everyone at the Circle T and prayed they'd be all right.

And Cord. A sob choked the back of her throat. God, she wished they hadn't argued earlier. She buried her head in her arms. If that twister met him coming back from town—she glanced over at her battered truck—he might not be as lucky as she was. Fear sliced through her like a jagged knife. He would be fine. He had to be.

She rolled onto her back, grimacing at the pain that sprinted up her arm where she'd slammed into the boulder. Her arms were scratched and bleeding and her jeans were torn at the knee, the skin scrapped underneath. The worst was over. All she had to do was lay here a moment and catch her breath before she started back to the ranch on foot.

That's when the blackness overhead opened up and it started to rain like hell.

Cord flipped on his windshield wipers, but as hard as it was raining, he knew they would do little good. He'd seen the tornado as it had swung north, toward the ranch, and though he was worried about the Circle T and the people there, there was nothing he could do about it.

Rachel was the only thing on his mind now. The thought of her out here, alone, facing a twister and now this storm made his chest tighten with dread....

A large black object caught his eye. Rachel's truck! His heart picked up speed, then nearly stopped when he saw that the vehicle lay on its side, the front windshield shattered.

The back wheels of his pickup skidded in the soft, wet dirt when Cord slammed on the brakes. Blood pounded in his temples as he pictured her slim, soft body inside the cab, broken like a porcelain doll's. He shouted her name as he jumped out of his truck and jerked open her cab door.

It was empty. Relief surged through his body and the rain battered his face as he lifted his head in thanks.

Where was she?

Cord swung around, searching the area through squinted eyes. The rain was so thick, it was hard to see. He swiped a hand over his face as if to wipe the water away, but it did no good.

"Rachel!"

He screamed her name as loud as he could and took a few steps, unsure of which way to go.

Damn! If he hadn't lost his temper with her this morning and been so preoccupied, he would have recognized the warning signs early. He would have got to her in time. If anything happened to her—

No. She was fine. He couldn't think otherwise. All this time he hadn't wanted to admit it to himself, but she was too precious to lose. He couldn't lose her. He *wouldn't* lose her.

He called to her again and again. It felt as if he were standing under a waterfall. The mud sucked at his boots as he took a few more steps to the left, desperately trying to see through the downpour. Through the pounding rhythm of the rain he heard a sound...a high-pitched voice....

Rachel!

He saw her then, weaving toward him as she stepped out of a ditch. He gave a shout of joy and ran to her, wrapping his arms around her as she stumbled toward him. She was covered with mud and her hair and clothes were drenched.

She'd never looked more beautiful.

"Are you all right?" he yelled over the storm.

She nodded. "I'm fine. Just get me out of here, please."

Cord swept her up in his arms and carried her to the truck. The rest was a blur for Rachel: the roar of the engine, the swish of the windshield wipers, a blanket being wrapped around her shoulders, then a rush of warm air from the heater. She closed her eyes tightly and buried her head in Cord's wet shoulder, trying to block out the image of the twister bearing down on her.

She opened her eyes suddenly and snapped her head up. "Cord, my truck—"

The tail winds buffeted the cab and Rachel was jerked to the other side of the seat. Still dripping, Cord reached over and buckled her into the seat belt. "Never mind your damn truck," he said tightly. "All that matters is you're safe."

He'd been worried about her, she realized. *Really* worried. Tears gathered in her eyes at the intensity of his words. White-knuckled, he gripped the steering wheel with both hands and concentrated on the road ahead. The rain was so hard, they could see no more than a few feet in front of them.

"What I was going to say—" she pulled the blanket higher around her shoulders "—was that the miserable machine stalled on me again. That's how I got stuck out here."

Cord swore through his clenched jaw. "I should have taken the keys and flushed them."

She tolerated the chiding because she deserved it. "You were right, Cord. I shouldn't have driven it." She sighed and leaned her head back against the seat. "I admit I can be . . . stubborn at times."

"You mean bullheaded, mulish and obstinate."

She screwed up her face at him. "You're pushing it now, cowboy."

They inched their way back to the ranch, with only the sound of the windshield wipers and the pounding of the rain on the roof of the cab. When they finally pulled up in front of the house, she reached for the door handle and started to open it.

"I've got to go check on Sam and Judy, make sure everyone is all right. The animals—"

"You're not going anywhere." He grabbed her wrist. "We'll call from the house and if we can't get ahold of them then *I* will go check on things."

"But—"

"Did I neglect to say pigheaded, headstrong and uncooperative?" His eyes narrowed. "Just keep it buttoned and for once, do what I say."

She clamped her mouth shut and stared at him.

"That's better."

He carried her into the house, kicking open the bathroom door as he headed for the shower. Closing the toilet lid, Cord set Rachel down there. She was shivering inside the blanket. The faucet squeaked when he turned on the hot water. "Let's get you in here."

She shook her head ardently. "Not until you call Sam."

He swore, then let out a long breath. "All right, I'll go call Sam. You better be sitting right here when I get back."

She lifted her chin and tightened the blanket around her, but said nothing. When he returned two minutes later, she was still sitting on the commode.

"Everyone is fine, including the animals."

Thank God. Rachel closed her eyes in relief.

"Now, Miss Difficult—I missed that one earlier— we've got to get you out of these clothes." He lifted her to a standing position and kissed her mud-streaked cheek. "Normally I'd be more than happy to do that myself, but it's going to be hard because you're so wet. You've got to help me."

She nodded weakly and let the blanket fall. Her fingers shook as she started on her shirt buttons, but Cord brushed her hands aside and in one motion yanked the shirt open. Buttons bounced on the tile floor. While he pulled her shirt off, she unsnapped her jeans and started to peel them down. When she nearly fell over, he made her sit on the toilet again and tugged them off himself.

"Did anyone ever tell you blue is a lovely color on you, darlin'?"

She frowned at him and he laughed, then stood her up and set her in the shower. Clouds of steam billowed into the bathroom. Eyes closed, she leaned against the tile wall, letting the hot water stimulate her skin and warm her inside. One minute later, Cord stepped in, naked, and pulled her into his arms. She laid her cheek against his bare chest, enjoying the feel of his hard body on the front side of her and the stinging hot water on her back. He kissed the top of her head and ran his hands over her back, as if to soothe her. Gradually she felt the tension ease out of her body.

It felt good to let someone take care of her like this. Rachel had never experienced this kind of tenderness or concern before. Her mother had always been too busy and Michael...well, Michael just wasn't the type.

After a few minutes, Cord shut off the water, toweled them both dry, then carried her into the bedroom. When she flinched as he set her on the edge of the bed, he frowned and knelt down in front of her.

"Are you hurt?"

"I—I'm not sure. My arm is sore and my knee burns."

Starting with her feet, Cord slowly worked his way up her leg. Numerous bruises dotted her legs and her left knee was scraped, as were her knuckles and elbows. When he touched her left arm, she cried out and jerked it back.

"What happened?" he asked grimly.

"I was chasing a rabbit." Rachel looked down at her arm. It was swelling rapidly, and a huge black-and-blue mark stared back at her.

He narrowed his eyes at her and frowned.

She sighed. "Unless I wanted to find out how it feels to be tossed in a food processor, I had to get out of the way fast. A ditch was the only place to go and I dove in without questioning what was at the bottom." She sucked in a breath of air when he gently touched her upper arm.

Wrapping a towel around his hips, Cord rose stiffly and walked to the closet. He stared at her clothes for a long moment, then reached out and tugged her robe off a hanger. She watched as he stood there, with his back still to her, her robe gripped tightly in his fist.

"Cord," she asked quietly, "what's wrong?"

Cord stared down at the robe in his hands. He could smell the scent of rose in the air, Rachel's scent, and he heard the storm as it pommeled the metal roof on the patio outside the French doors.

But the storm raging outside was nothing compared to what was raging inside of him. He'd never experienced this kind of emotion, an aching so profound, so frighteningly intense, he thought his chest might rip in two.

He turned slowly and looked at her sitting on the edge of the bed, her hair dripping wet. She looked so fragile, so delicate. His throat felt strangely thick.

"What's wrong?" he repeated, his voice almost a whisper. His knuckles were white where he clutched the robe. "You almost died."

Rachel met Cord's hard gaze, stunned by the stark emotion she'd just heard in his voice. There was pain there. And fear. Her heart lurched in her chest and her breath caught. They were moving into uncharted territory here and she wanted to proceed cautiously. "I didn't," she answered carefully. "I'm here."

His body was coiled tight, like wire, and she sensed whatever it was he was trying to control was tearing him up inside. When he moved beside her, his hands were clenched into fists at his sides. She tugged the robe from his fingers and tossed it on the bed, then stood and wrapped her arms around his neck. He tensed at her touch.

"Cord," she whispered, pressing her lips to his chest, "I need you to hold me."

He closed his eyes tightly and kept his arms stiffly at his sides. "I'm afraid I'll hurt you," he said, his voice ragged.

She laughed softly. "I just survived a tornado, cowboy. I think I can survive you, too."

His arms came around her then, fiercely, yet gently. She clung to him and pressed herself closer. His lips brushed her temple, then her cheek. "When I saw your truck lying on its side, it was like someone pulling barbwire through my gut."

She ran her hands over his damp skin and his muscles bunched under her fingers. "I'm fine. Just a little scared, that's all."

He lifted her off the floor and buried his face in her neck. "That makes two of us."

Rachel tried to sort out the rush of emotions careening through her at the moment. Though she and Cord had spent the past month together as husband and wife in the physical sense, there'd been no talk of commitment or love. Nothing to suggest he might stay at the end of the year.

She didn't want to misunderstand what was happening between them right now. Desperately, she longed to tell him how much she loved him, how much she needed him. He had told her he wasn't the marrying kind, that he had no intention of ever being tied down. But he was talking to her now, sharing his feelings with her. This was the first step they'd taken beyond sex or business.

But if she moved too quickly, told him how she felt, would he grab his saddle and run?

She couldn't take that chance. Not now. She'd show him how much she loved him. Tell him with her body. He'd have to know, he'd have to feel it. It was too strong for him not to.

She took his face in her hands and stroked his lips with her thumbs. "Make love to me, Cord," she said softly, pressing her lips to his.

He groaned deep in his throat and closed his eyes. "God, Rachel, I want to, but what you've just been through, and your arm is—"

"Is fine." She stopped him with another kiss. "And I'll be fine, but only if you make love to me. Soon."

They sank to the bed slowly, but he twisted at the last minute and pulled her on top of him. She knew he was worried he might hurt her and her heart swelled at the tenderness with which he kissed her. But he was holding back, and she didn't want that. She wanted all of him, body and soul.

She urged him with her hands and her tongue, moving over him slowly and seductively. His skin was hot now and she tasted him, his lips, his neck, then down to his chest and farther still to the flat, solid planes of his flat stomach. She made love to him, reveling in the response her touch invoked. His sharp intake of breath encouraged her, and when he called her name she thought her heart might burst with the love she felt for him.

She rose, then lowered herself on top of him, closing her eyes as the painful ache inside of her turned to intense pleasure. He touched her breasts, then grasped her hips as she moved, calling out her name. The need built, higher and stronger, until the first tremor seized her, then ripped through her like a bolt of lightning. Cord drove himself hard into her, shuddering as the force of his climax shook his body.

She'd never known such joy, such an overwhelming sense of completion. She thought she might cry from sheer happiness. A moment later, as he pulled her gently into his arms, she did.

Nine

"**G**et back in that bed."

Rachel jumped at the sound of Cord's voice from the bedroom door. She thought he was out checking the damage from yesterday's storm. She gave him a wicked smile as she stood and snapped the button on her jeans. "It's lonely in here."

One corner of his mouth turned up before he frowned again and moved beside her. "You promised me you'd stay in bed today."

She laid her hands on his chest and slid her arms around his neck. "That's when I thought you'd be with me."

"I'm here now." He pulled her against him and kissed her hard.

Rachel returned the kiss and she could feel herself melting all over again, wanting him and never having enough. They'd fallen asleep late last night, in each other's arms, with the storm still raging outside. This morning, when they'd awakened, the sky was clear and the smell of rain hung heavy in the air.

Difficult as it was, she pulled away from him. "You're too late, Cantrell. I'm out of bed now and dressed."

"We can correct that," he said, backing her toward the bed. "I've been hard all morning just thinking about you lying up here, naked."

He tried to nibble on her neck, but she sidestepped him and reached for a boot as she sat on the edge of the mattress. "I've got to go see for myself how the ranch fared. That hole in the barn roof must have leaked like a waterfall."

Cord was quiet for a moment, then he cleared his throat. "You don't have to worry about that hole in the roof anymore."

She tugged on a boot. "What do you mean, not worry about it? After that storm? There had to be some damage."

He sat down beside her on the bed. "You don't have to worry about it, because the barn no longer has a roof."

Boot in hand, she froze. What was he talking about, no roof? He must be kidding. She glanced over at him and the somber look in his eyes told her he wasn't.

Her heart sank and she had an awful feeling she didn't want to hear this. She closed her eyes and took a deep breath. "What...what happened?"

He took her hand and twisted her fingers in his. "The tornado sucked it right off. The walls and everything inside are intact, but there's one hell of a skylight at the moment."

She lay her head on his shoulder and let out a long sigh. "What else?"

"That's it. Nothing else was touched."

The truck and the barn roof. How was she ever going to replace them? The ranch was barely squeaking by each month and now this. A balloon of frustration welled up in her. She *had* the money, she just couldn't get her hands on it with Earl blocking her way. *Damn* her brother-in-law and the control he had over her, and damn Michael for giving him that rein.

Suddenly she lifted her head and stared at Cord. "You knew about this yesterday?"

"Well, yes, but—"

She jerked her hand out of his and stood. "And you didn't tell me?"

His expression hardened. "Rachel, you'd just been through a trauma, you needed to rest. And besides, what could you have done?"

"Whether I could have done anything or not isn't the point. I have a right to know." Standing, she yanked on her second boot, nearly falling over as a wave of dizziness washed over her.

Cord's hands were on her shoulders instantly, steadying her. "That's exactly *my* point," he said sharply, setting her back on the bed. "You're still weak as a newborn foal. You have no business being out of this bed."

"My *business* is my ranch." She pressed a hand to her temple, waiting for the nausea to pass. "Everything that happens here concerns me. Just because I'm a little sore, and a little tired, doesn't mean I'm helpless or defenseless."

Cord's jaw was clenched tight when she looked back up at him. "No one ever said you were."

"No?" She straightened her shoulders and stood. "Then why didn't you tell me?"

"I didn't want you any more upset than you already were. I thought I was doing the right thing."

It was too much. The months of struggling to hold on to the ranch, worrying about money. She felt a bubble of hysteria rise in her chest.

"The right thing?" She faced him and narrowed her eyes. "Michael thought he was doing the right thing when he left my finances to Earl. Earl says *he's* doing the right thing by refusing to hand over to me what's rightfully mine. And Raskin, the idiot, told me I'd thank him some day for turning down my loan."

"I don't like you comparing me with them." His voice was tight, edged with controlled anger.

"Oh, Cord, I'm not comparing you to them." Sighing, she took a step toward him. "You talked to me about attitudes before. Well, I'm sick to death of men's attitudes, this damn notion they have that I need protecting. I don't need protecting. I'm perfectly capable of taking care of myself."

"I'll keep that in mind," he said flatly.

He was hurt, Rachel knew that, but how was she ever going to make him understand how *she* felt? She had to try. "Cord," she said softly, "if you were in my shoes, how would *you* feel? Wouldn't you want to know if something had happened, whether it was bad or good? And as long as you could still breathe, would you be sitting around in bed letting other people take care of you?"

He folded his arms. "Of course not."

"Exactly." She laid her hands on his arms. "I know my limits, Cord. I'm not so foolish to push myself over the edge. But even if I do, that's my decision. I'll just have to learn how to pick myself up again.''

She felt her heart begin to sink as he stared at her, his jaw clenched and his lips pressed tightly together. He wasn't going to even try to understand, she thought miserably. If he didn't, there'd be no hope at all for them.

A long, tense moment passed before he drew in a deep breath and let it out again. Then his arms came around her and he pulled her against him. Rachel closed her eyes in relief, feeling as if a slab of cement had just been lifted off her chest.

''Cord.'' She bit her lip. It wasn't the best of times to approach the next subject, but she had no choice.

''What?''

His hands were sliding down her back, making it difficult to concentrate. ''I was wondering . . . when's the next futurity?''

''Next Saturday, in Abilene,'' he answered, then stilled. ''Why?''

''Well—'' she shrugged ''—if the prize money was big enough, and if I was lucky enough, then it might cover the cost of a new roof.''

His face was a tight mask as he released her. ''You can't possibly make that one. You need some time to heal. I can enter, though. The purse on this one is a good sum and I'm sure it will cover—''

Rachel shook her head. ''We've been through this, Cord. I can't take your money.''

She could see the fury in his eyes, but she wouldn't let him intimidate her. ''Please,'' she said, lifting her gaze to his, ''let me try it my way.''

A muscle jumped at the back of Cord's jaw. He nodded stiffly. ''Okay, Rachel. We'll try it your way.''

He stared at her another moment. "But if it doesn't work, then we do it mine."

Holding a wet paper towel to her face, Rachel stepped out of the bathroom stall at the fairgrounds. She paused, drew in a deep breath, then washed her hands and finger-combed her hair before placing her hat back on her head.

It was the third go-around for the show today. So far, she'd just managed to squeak by and stay in it. If she scored high today, she'd advance to the finals.

She stared at her reflection in the mirror and frowned. Her skin was paler today than it had been and she felt a little shaky. Though it was normal for her to lose her breakfast before a competition, she felt weaker than usual. Her head was pounding like a jackhammer, also. She pulled the brim of her hat low. Maybe Cord wouldn't notice.

Like hell he wouldn't. He'd been watching her like a hawk since the twister had hit. Just waiting for her to fall apart. He hadn't wanted her to enter this competition and she wondered if maybe he were right. Though her cuts and scrapes had healed, she'd had less strength this past week, not to mention an occasional bout of dizziness.

She hadn't dared to tell him, though. There'd been enough tension between them. The only time that tension was set aside was at night, when they went to bed. The bedroom was the one place they did not bring their differences. She'd sensed an urgency in Cord's lovemaking since the tornado hit. A desperation almost. As if he couldn't get enough of her. Or maybe, she thought bleakly, he was trying to get her out of his system. Have his fill, so to speak, before he moved on. Since the day of the twister, nothing had been said about the future, or what he felt for her.

What would happen to her if she allowed herself to become emotionally and physically dependent on him? How would she ever pick herself back up again and continue on as before?

She was kidding herself to think that she could. It was going to hurt when he left, and that's all there was to it. She'd deal with it. She had to.

When she stepped out of the bathroom, Cord was leaning against the outside wall, his arms folded. Concern etched the fine lines around his blue eyes. She was going to get a lecture, she knew it. She forced a spring into her step as she approached him.

"Where's Sam?" she asked. Her foreman had come along this trip to cheer her and Cord to victory.

Cord nodded toward the arena. "He wanted a front-row seat to watch you."

Rachel laughed. "You mean so he could shout instructions."

Cord smiled, then reached out and tipped her hat back. He frowned. "You were sick again, weren't you?" he said sharply.

"Of course I was. I always get sick before I ride, you know that." She forced a bright smile. "That's how I win."

Pushing away from the wall, Cord frowned at her. "I've never seen you this pale before."

"I'm fine, Cord, really." She glanced at her watch, then spotted Montana tied to a fence post a few feet away. "It's about time for me to mount up. Is Montana ready?"

"A hell of a lot more ready than you are."

She felt the stab of his words, but was determined not to let him get to her. The hammering in her head increased. "Whatever happened to 'winning's an attitude, darlin'"? You're supposed to be wishing me luck, not shooting my confidence to smithereens." She turned and walked toward the horse.

He followed. "You don't belong out there today, Rachel."

"You mean *you* don't want me out there." She stopped and he practically ran into her.

"That's right, dammit," he said loudly, attracting the attention of several bystanders milling around. He lowered his voice when Rachel glared at him. "Call it any way you want, but I sure as hell am not going to wish you luck to go break your neck."

"Don't be ridiculous." She lifted her foot into the stirrup and hoisted herself into the saddle. "I'm perfectly all right. I've done well the last two days, haven't I? Why should today be different?"

"I don't know why." His expression softened. "I just know it is."

She reached down and kissed his cheek. "I appreciate your concern, Cord. Really. But I'm fine."

His features tightened, but he said nothing.

The buzzer signaled the rider just before Rachel. She adjusted her hat, checked her stirrup length, then urged Montana toward the ring.

One more ride, Rachel told herself as she entered the ring. One more, then we go for the biggie. She blinked her eyes to clear away the white spots there and sucked in a deep breath.

Her heart pounding, Rachel waited for the announcer to call her name.

When the buzzer sounded, she moved toward the herd, then through it to split the animals up. Deciding on a feisty-looking tan-colored cow, Rachel swung Montana sharply to the left, letting the horse know which cow to focus on.

The cow broke right. So did Montana. Rachel held on, moving with the horse. The crowd cheered, praising the clean cut, but to Rachel, it sounded as if she were in a tin drum. Her head felt suddenly light. As she felt herself slipping, she grabbed frantically for the saddle horn, but her fingers turned to liquid and she lost her grip.

Then there was nothing.

Cord watched helplessly as Rachel fell from the saddle. His heart slammed in his chest as he ran toward her, calling out her name as she hit the soft dirt, her limp body now in the path of an anxious cow. Cord yelled and waved his arms, frightening the calf off, then scooped Rachel up and carried her out of the arena, beneath the shade of an oak. He laid her carefully down on a patch of soft grass. Sam was beside him in a second, as were a few other concerned bystanders.

"Rachel!"

Her eyes fluttered when he called her name.

His fingers were shaking as he brushed the hair away from her face. Her skin was pale and clammy. "Wake up, honey."

Someone handed him a cold, wet cloth and he pressed it to her forehead. She moaned softly, then opened her eyes.

"What . . . what happened?"

"You fainted." He wiped the rag over her cheeks and neck.

"Don't be silly." She frowned at him. "I don't faint."

"All right, then—" he accepted the water Sam handed him and lifted her head so she could have a drink "—you fell asleep in the middle of a cut."

She took a sip of the water, then brushed it aside. "This is hardly the time for jokes, Cantrell." Sitting, she lifted a shaky hand to her forehead and closed her eyes.

"Nor is it the time for you to be so damn stubborn. Lay back down until the paramedics get here."

Her eyes flew open. "Paramedics! I just got a little dizzy, for heaven's sake. I don't need a paramedic."

Did she need anyone? he wondered, gritting his teeth. The pounding fear in Cord's chest was slowly changing to anger. "You argue with me, woman, so help me, I'll tie you up and throw you in the back of the horse trailer with Montana. Now you lay down and as soon as the paramedics check you out then Sam here is going to take you back to the hotel."

"Back to the hotel! Cord, I can't miss your ride—"

"Sam," Cord said over his shoulder, "get me my rope out of my trailer, would you?"

She stilled and her eyes, angry and wide, met his. "You would, wouldn't you?"

"Damn straight." He didn't flinch.

Furious, Rachel folded her arms and lay back down. Her lips were locked tightly together and she refused to look at him.

Blast her pigheadedness, Cord thought, stepping out of the way as the paramedics arrived. Though he'd come to understand that stubborn streak in her, maybe even admire it, it still aggravated the hell out of him. He curled his fingers into fists as he watched one paramedic wrap a blood-pressure cuff around Rachel's arm while the other checked her eyes and pulse. She could have been seriously hurt out there, or worse, if those cows had stampeded.

"How is she?" Cord asked the man who had taken Rachel's blood pressure.

"Appears to be fine," he commented, tucking the instrument back into his bag. Rachel sat up, then glared at Cord and lifted her chin in an I-told-you-so gesture. He ignored her.

"She had a bad fall a week ago," Cord said. "Could this be related?"

He shrugged. "Unless she hit her head, most likely not. Looks to me like nerves and the heat, but it wouldn't hurt to get her checked out anyway. You can give a copy of our report to the doctor."

"Thanks. We'll do that." Cord signaled to the announcer that Rachel was fine and the crowd clapped for her. She closed her eyes in embarrassment.

Cord turned to Sam. "Would you mind taking Rachel back to the hotel now, Sam?"

"Be happy to." Sam stepped forward and held out his hand to Rachel. She hesitated, then sighed in resignation and let her foreman help her up.

"We'll talk about this later, Cord," Rachel whispered between clenched teeth.

"Bet on it." He nodded slowly.

Her shoulders squared, Rachel aimed a look at him that could kill, then turned and marched away. Brows raised, Sam touched the brim of his hat to Cord and followed her.

When they were out of sight, Cord released a long, weary breath, thankful that she hadn't called his hand. He *would* have tied her up and dragged her back to the hotel—against her will, if necessary. Someone had to make her take a step back and take a look at what she was doing to herself.

She was sleeping less, working harder and her worry over losing the ranch was eating her up inside.

Still, she refused his help financially.

Why? he wondered, trying to force down the frustration rising in his chest. Why was it so difficult for her to accept his assistance? He was her *husband*.

But he wasn't, was he? He turned stiffly and made his way back to retrieve Montana. Rachel had made it clear from the beginning she didn't want—or need—a husband, other than to gain control of her trust back from Earl. And even marriage hadn't helped her do that.

So what good was he to her, other than pleasure in bed and working the horses?

Cord yanked Montana's reins free from the post he'd been tied to, adjusted the stirrups and pulled himself up in the saddle. Maybe he should have let her marry someone else. There would have been other men who would have fit the bill. Why had be been so intent on taking the "job"? Though he'd told himself it was for the land, he knew damn well it wasn't.

From the first time he'd laid eyes on Rachel, he'd wanted her. Maybe at first it was just in bed, but then—*now*—now he wanted all of her. He wanted a *real* wife and he wanted to be a real husband, one she would come to with her problems, share her joys with.

Have some kids.

He shook his head at the thought. He'd never imagined himself with a wife or kids. Ranch life was hard, the hours long and the money uncertain. Cord remembered the unhappiness he'd seen in his own mother, the long hours of silence, the tears of loneliness. He'd never considered putting a woman through that.

But Rachel wasn't his mother—he knew that. He'd seen the love in Rachel's eyes for the land—her land—and he'd come to understand the passion she felt. The Circle T, and Rachel, had worked their way into his blood, his heart, and they were as important to him as breathing. He wanted to help her keep the ranch, work it with her.

Who was he kidding? Cord swung Montana around and headed for the stables. Rachel didn't want that. He'd fallen in love with a woman who was hell-bent on proving to the world she could make it without a man.

Fallen in love. It hit him like a two-by-four in the chest. Wasn't that a laugh? Cord Cantrell in love. The words, as well as the feeling, were foreign to him.

He needed some time to get used to the idea. Make sure it would fit. He wasn't sure he liked the concept, but a man certainly didn't throw a new pair of boots away just because they rubbed at him. He gave them some time to break in.

He and Rachel were going to talk. He'd told her he'd try it her way, but it hadn't worked for him.

It was time to do things his way.

"Sam, I appreciate you bringing me back here, but really, you don't have to stay. I know you came to watch Cord ride and sitting here baby-sitting me is not necessary."

Rachel paced the length of the hotel patio that overlooked the pool. It had cooled down some and the fresh air renewed her. She felt better than she had in a long time—other than the fact she was so mad at Cord, she could spit.

"I don't mind." Sam spread his long legs out in front of him and crossed his boots at the ankle. "I reckon the view here is ten times prettier than watching your husband cavort with some cow."

Rachel followed the direction of Sam's gaze and frowned. The lounge chairs by the pool held several young ladies clad in provocative swimsuits. Pausing, she put her hands on her hips and tilted her head disapprovingly. "Shame on you. What would Judy say about you drooling over some bathing beauties?"

He grinned. "Long as my heart don't give out, I reckon she wouldn't mind. Lookin's not touchin', and when you've been through as much together as we have, you learn not to sweat the small stuff."

"Sometimes it's hard to sort out the small from the big." She turned to look down at the crystal-blue water in the pool. "I've been a little...uptight lately."

"You've taken a lot on those pretty little shoulders of yours," Sam said. "Might be easier for you if you let those people who care about you help a little more."

Rachel sighed. "Oh, Sam. Not you, too. I thought you might be the one man who understood what the Circle T means to me."

"I understand, all right. More than you think." He rose and came to stand beside her, grasping the iron rail of the patio as he looked down. "Cord wants to help, Rachel. Real bad. Being he's your husband, you might think about letting him."

Rachel glanced over at Sam. He'd been her friend for two years. If she couldn't trust him, then she couldn't trust anyone. She hesitated a moment, then drew in a deep breath. "What if I told you that Cord and I aren't really married?"

Sam's brows rose. "How's that?"

She hurried on, "Oh, we're legally married, all right. I mean we're not married like you and Judy."

She folded her arms and looked out at the horizon where blue Texas sky met the flat, rugged range of Abilene. "When Michael died, he left a stipulation in his will that my inheritance be left in the form of a trust, with his brother as administrator, until I remarried."

"Why would he do that?" Sam asked, furrowing his forehead.

"It was his own convoluted way of making sure I had a man to take care of me, to protect me from making frivolous financial investments and losing the money."

"You? Frivolous?" Sam gave a bark of laughter.

"Thanks. I needed that." She covered his hand with her own. "But Michael never saw me as anything other than a fragile, vulnerable woman who was incapable of making a decision past which color nail polish to wear."

"Shoot, you don't even wear nail polish."

Rachel smiled. "I was falling behind in my bills and when the last trainer quit, I became desperate. I hired a private investigator to find me a husband and Cord's name was on the list. I asked him to marry me and work on the ranch training horses for one year, at which time I would grant him a divorce and one thousand acres of land. He'll be free to go his way then, and so will I."

As if she could ever really be free of Cord. His smile flashed in her mind, his blue eyes, his hands touching her, loving her.... He'd always be with her, even when he was gone, and she knew she'd never be free.

"Who would have thought?" Sam shook his head. "You getting married to save the ranch. Sounds like one of those movies for TV."

Rachel frowned. Sam seemed to be taking this news awfully calmly. "Yeah. Who would have thought?"

Scratching his chin, Sam furrowed his brow and looked at her. "So what's the problem?"

"What's the problem?" Rachel threw her hands up and resumed her pacing. All the pain, all the frustration of the past two years bubbled their way to the surface. She felt an ache in her chest and a pounding in her head. All the hard work, the sacrifice ... for what? The ranch was slipping through her fingers like sand and she was helpless to stop it.

Helpless. The word made her throat constrict. She wasn't, dammit, she *wasn't.*

"I'll tell you what the problem is," she said bitterly. "All my life, starting with my father, I've been sheltered and protected from all the terrible things that can happen to a woman out in the big bad world. Michael also felt it his supreme masculine duty to shield me from life's malevolence and now Earl is pressuring me to sell the ranch by holding back what is rightfully mine.

"What I don't need—" she folded her arms "—and I don't want, is another man hovering over me, telling me what to do or how to live my life."

Rachel froze. A slight sound from the doorway made her turn and she stared into Cord's cold blue eyes. His mouth was set firmly, his shoulders stiff as stone.

Sam also turned at that moment and nodded to the younger man. "Cord. How'd you do?"

"I lost." Cord's gaze stayed riveted on Rachel.

"Too bad." Sam cleared his throat, then picked up his hat and slapped it on his head. "If you two don't mind, I think I'll just mosey on down to the pool. My eyesight's not as good as it used to be."

After Sam left, the silence stretched uncomfortably, until Rachel finally spoke. "I'm . . . sorry you lost."

"We both did."

She suddenly had the strangest feeling he wasn't talking about the competition. "How much of my conversation did you hear?"

A muscle jumped in his jaw. "Enough."

"Cord—"

"What's it going to be, Rachel?"

Confused, she lowered her brows. "What do you mean?"

"A man's pride can only stand so much. I've let you call the shots because that's what we agreed to before we got married. But things have changed now. Maybe acting the part of husband for this long has started to make me feel like one. Maybe my pride just won't let me be led around by the nose anymore. Or maybe I just care too much about you to stand around with my hands tied and let you do harm to yourself."

"What are you talking about, 'do harm to myself'?"

"I'm talking about your truck breaking down and you nearly being killed."

"But—"

"And I'm talking about you falling off a horse in a dead faint during a competition. I knew you weren't up to that ride and you knew it, too. Because I told you no, you made sure you went out there, just to prove a point. How many cows would have to stampede over you before you had some sense pounded into you?''

He swiped an angry hand through the air. "No more. You've carried this 'I don't need a man' scenario to its limit with me. You want to make decisions? Fine. Then make this one—either I stay, and we do it my way, or I leave."

Leave? Cord leave? She started to reach out to him, desperate to make him understand how she felt, but then she stopped. He was intimidating her, trying to bully her into submission. She could never let another man do that to her.

Not even Cord.

"And just what exactly does doing it *your* way mean?" She folded her arms so he wouldn't see them shaking. "Complete obedience on my part? Total acquiescence?"

His eyes narrowed. "If that's what it takes to save you from making mistakes."

"Oh, yes," she said sarcastically. "I'd nearly forgotten the fairy tale. Big brave male saves incompetent, fragile female. I'm supposed to fall at your feet and thank you now."

She lifted her chin, refusing to give in to the tears burning at the back of her throat. "I've got news for you, Cantrell. I don't need you to save me from anything."

Cord's face hardened and he clenched his fists tightly at his sides. "Okay, Rachel, you've made your decision, then. I know a couple of trainers unhappy with the ranches they're working on. I'll send one over to take my place.''

She cursed her own stubborn pride that refused to allow her to tell him not to leave, that she'd do it his way if only he'd stay. But she couldn't. She couldn't beg him to stay, knuckle under to him. How could she face herself if she did?

"Don't bother," she said tersely. "I've still got my list from before."

A cold glint filled his eyes. "Fine. I'll let you know where you can send my things."

Without a word, he turned. Rachel heard a drawer open, then slam closed, but she couldn't see through the blur of tears. This couldn't really be happening.

I love you, Cord. Can't you see? Please don't go.

When the door slammed, she could no longer hold her tears in. Her knees buckled under her and she sank to the patio floor, quietly sobbing his name. She'd never felt so miserably alone in her life.

Cord had been right earlier. They *had* both lost.

Ten

———

"**I**'m what?"

Numb, Rachel stared at Dr. Roberts as he made notations in the chart on his desk. He'd been her doctor for the two years she'd been living in Sweetwater, but she'd only seen him twice professionally. Once for a sprained wrist and once for an eye infection. He glanced up at her over the rim of his thick glasses and smiled.

"You're fit as spinach and apples," he said, repeating his vegetarian appraisal of her health.

"No, not that part. What you said before." Her heart was pounding so fast, she had to grip the arms of her chair.

"That you're pregnant?" He furrowed his brow. "I assumed you knew that when you had your lab work done three days ago."

Pregnant? She raised a trembling hand to her face and felt the icy touch of her cheek. How could she be pregnant? She and Cord had been careful every time.

Except once.

The first time. That was the one, the only time, they'd made love and used no protection. But she'd thought for sure it was safe that particular day.

"You mean you *didn't* know?" The doctor raised his brows.

She shook her head slowly. "I—I came in for the tests because I've been a little dizzy and tired all the time. I missed one period, but that's not unusual for me when I'm under a lot of pressure. I thought that's all it was—stress."

Dr. Robert's eyes narrowed with concern. "What kind of stress?"

What kind of stress? A laugh bordering on the hysterical stuck like a lump of clay in her throat. Cord had been gone for a week with no word. Parker was training the horses as best he could, while she and the other hands took up the slack. She worked until she was too exhausted to move, then she cried herself to sleep every night.

That kind of stress.

But she couldn't tell the doctor that. "I'm short-handed at the ranch, plus I lost my truck and barn roof to the tornado."

"I heard about that, Rachel. I'm sorry."

She nodded. Small towns hear about everything. It wouldn't be long before everyone knew her husband had left, too. She suddenly felt tired. Tired of putting up a front, tired of working and sacrificing. All for what? An empty bed and an upset stomach. Without Cord, none of it seemed to matter anymore.

Except the baby.

She touched her stomach, marveling at the thought. A baby. *Her* baby. She absorbed the word, ran it over and over in her mind.

Slowly, incredibly, an excitement began to dance through her. As much as she'd wanted children, she had thought it would be a few more years before she started a family. She'd never considered having a child now.

Or had she?

Was it possible that loving Cord as she did, that after he'd left she would want something of his, of theirs? Something that no one could take away? Hadn't she known in her heart that after Cord was gone there would never be anyone else?

All the warning signs of her pregnancy had been there, but she'd chosen to ignore them, afraid to admit even to herself how desperately she wanted Cord and herself to be a genuine, bona fide family. No agreement, no business deal, but truly husband and wife. Two people who loved and cared about each other, who shared not only a bed, but joys and sorrows.

And responsibilities.

She'd never given Cord a chance to share anything more than a bed, she realized now. All he'd ever wanted to do was help her, but she'd been hell-bent on proving that she could do it alone.

And now she was.

God, how she missed him. She wondered where he was right now, what he was doing. An ache of loneliness spread over her as she glanced over at the empty chair beside her, trying to imagine Cord's face as the doctor told them she was pregnant. Would he be happy, or angry? She didn't even know how he felt about children, if he liked them or not. The subject had never come up and babies had definitely not been part of their agreement.

But then neither had falling in love. She could still hear Cord's voice. *Winnin's an attitude, darlin'. Anticipate. Let yourself feel it.* She closed her eyes and the only thing she could feel was the pain of losing him. It sliced through her, cutting her into a thousand pieces. For two years all she wanted was the Circle T, a place to call home and raise a family. Now, with Cord gone, it no longer seemed to matter where she lived.

All that mattered was the baby.

"Rachel?"

Dr. Roberts was standing beside her, gently touching her shoulder. She was suddenly aware that tears were streaming down her cheeks.

"I'm sorry if this isn't what you wanted, honey."

Isn't what she wanted? She gave a short laugh and wiped at her tears. "Doctor, I want this baby more than anything else in the entire world. You have no idea how happy I am."

"Well, then," he said cheerfully as he patted her on the shoulder. "let's talk about diet and vitamins. We want this little Cantrell to be the healthiest bouncing baby Sweetwater ever saw."

Rachel smiled, then felt a wave of panic. She grabbed the doctor by the arm. "Two weeks ago I got pretty well banged up during the tornado and a week ago I fell off a horse. My baby, I mean, will everything—"

"Rachel." He put a finger under her chin. "Look at me and listen. Your baby is fine. The Good Lord made babies tougher than you can imagine. Unless you've been spotting or had cramps—'' he hesitated, then smiled when she shook her head ''—then everything is fine and in about seven and a half months you'll be holding the little tyke. To be on the safe side, though, why don't you avoid horses and tornadoes till after he—or she—is born.''

Relief surged through her. *Seven and a half months.* The doctor began to rummage through his desk drawers. "Hold on a minute. I've got some reading material here on prenatal care. Just let me find it.''

She sat down again, but could barely keep still. She resolved not to think about her problems right now, there'd be plenty of time for that later. She was going to concentrate on the baby. On a nursery and clothes and diapers and a hundred other things she'd need to prepare. She couldn't wait to see Judy's face. She'd been lamenting no grandchildren from her boys yet and Rachel knew she'd be happy for her. Sam was gone for a couple of days visiting a brother in Dallas, so he'd have to wait for the news. Once Sam knew, she smiled, well, then everyone would know.

Everyone except Cord.

She closed her eyes, trying to hold back the hurt that invaded her. Even if he didn't love her, he had a right to know. It was his baby, too. She couldn't bear the thought of him coming back just because of the baby. Either he came back because he loved her, or she didn't want him back at all, no matter how deeply she loved him.

Sighing, she accepted the pamphlets the doctor handed her and forced herself to smile again. She didn't even know where Cord was, let alone how to get in touch with him. Maybe it was for the best. She needed some time right now to think this out before she told him. Time to sort through the situation.

There were decisions to be made, and this time she had to think of someone other than herself.

Whoever it was knocking at the hotel room door was damned persistent.

Cord struggled to open one eye, grimacing at the pain that small movement cost him. His head was screaming like a wood chipper and his mouth felt as if it were filled with sawdust. His cheek was pressed against something soft and scratchy. He lifted his head, then groaned as the continued knocking sounded in his head with the force of a jackhammer.

He opened his eyes and realized he was sleeping in an armchair. On his stomach, no less. His knees were jammed onto the hard floor, his head draped over the back. It wasn't possible to sleep that way.

Unless you were dead drunk.

Closing his eyes again, Cord let his head drop back down to the chair. His joints were too stiff to move. He doubted he could crawl to that door, much less open it. "Go away," he called out, but his throat was too dry for it to sound like anything other than an incoherent mumbling.

Slowly, painfully, he turned himself over, frowning when he realized he was fully dressed. The first few nights since he'd left Rachel he'd at least been able to get his pants off before he passed out. But each night it had taken just a little more whiskey to ease the ache and drown out the image of her soft and warm in their bed.

Her bed, he sharply reminded himself. *Her* ranch. *Her* life. A whiskey bottle sat two feet away from him, on the hotel room nightstand. He started to reach for it when the door opened.

"Hey, Cord, you up? It's me, Sam." The old man stuck his head in the door.

Sam. What the hell was he doing here? Cord struggled to sit up straight, trying to achieve what he hoped would be at least a little dignity. His feet slipped out from under him and he realized he was missing one boot and sock. So much for dignity.

He let his head roll back and closed his eyes.

Sam sat down on the bed across from Cord and held out a white paper bag. "Thought you might like some breakfast."

The idea of food made Cord's stomach reel threateningly. He shook his head, then held it still with his hands when he thought it might roll away. "What are you doing here, Sam?"

"Visiting a friend." He handed Cord a large paper cup. "Coffee?"

The first bright spot since Sam walked in. Muttering a thanks, Cord accepted the cup, grateful that the brew was hot and black. He lifted his head again, wincing at the effort, then sipped loudly.

Sam's gaze shifted from the whiskey bottle to Cord's bare foot. "Rough night?"

Cord ran a hand over his face. The bristle of a three-day-old beard scratched at his palm. "How did you find me?"

Sam shrugged. "Heard you signed up for a competition here in Dallas day after tomorrow. Just thought I'd stop in and say hello."

Cord sighed. "I appreciate your coming here, Sam, but I'm not coming back."

Shaking his head, Sam pulled a breakfast burger out of the bag beside him. "Shoot, I don't stick my nose where it don't belong. I just thought you might need a friend."

Cord reached over and grabbed the whiskey bottle. "I've got a friend." He unscrewed the cap with his teeth and poured a shot into his coffee.

"My granddaddy always said when one solution creates another problem, it ain't no solution." He opened the burger, smelled it, then shrugged and took a bite.

Cord watched a fat drop of grease drip off Sam's finger and felt his stomach pitch. "Your granddaddy wasn't married to Rachel."

Sam gave a snort of laughter. "I admit she's one determined lady. Sort of respect that quality myself."

"Determination I respect, also." Cord slugged down a mouthful of coffee, enjoying the bite of the whiskey mixed with the hot brew. "Reckless stupidity I do not."

The old man was thoughtful for a moment as he chewed a big bite. "Rachel told me," he said finally, " 'bout how you two got hitched so she could save the ranch."

Cord nodded. "I thought she might have."

"Seems like a shame for you both to go to all that trouble for nothing."

"It's not for nothing," Cord replied defensively. "Rachel needed a husband to gain control of her money. She's got a husband. Whether I live there or not shouldn't matter."

"Maybe." Sam took another bite. "But she still might lose the ranch."

"No." Cord sat straighter, his features hardening. "I won't let that happen. She might not want my help, but she's getting it anyway. I've already paid a contractor to fix the barn and spoken to Joe about sending me the bill when her truck's fixed. If she doesn't have another trainer within a week, then I'll send her one." He took a long pull on his coffee. Anger and frustration burned through him, freshly scorching those feelings he'd been trying to tamp down.

Sam nodded approvingly. "What about Earl? What if he tries to force her hand again and make her sell?"

"I'm working on that, too." Cord's eyes narrowed. "Rachel won't have to worry about him for too much longer."

Sam's brows raised. "You wouldn't be doing something foolish, would you, boy?"

"Foolish?" Cord's laugh was dry. "That's my middle name. But if you mean violence, no." He shook his head. "As much as I'd enjoy it, it won't be necessary."

"Sounds like you thought of everything." Sam dumped the rest of the burger into the bag and wiped his hands off on a napkin. " 'Cept for one thing."

"What?"

"Rachel." He stood and stuck his thumbs in the front loops of his jeans. "She loves you. How you gonna fix that one, cowboy?"

Rachel loves me? That was ridiculous. He shook his head. "The only thing Rachel loves is the ranch and making decisions all by herself." Cord reached for the whiskey bottle again and poured in another shot. "A man's pride can only stand so much, Sam. I can't come back to that."

"I expect you're right, son. You gotta do what you gotta do." He picked up his trash and pitched it into the plastic trash can in the corner. "I'll just be heading back to the ranch now. It's Wednesday so Judy'll be making my favorite meal tonight. Meat loaf."

When he turned, Cord felt an overwhelming desire to tell him to wait, that he'd come with him.

But he couldn't. He could only watch as the old man walked to the door and opened it.

"Just answer me this, Cord," Sam said, turning back around. "What would you do if Rachel were a horse?"

He smiled then and left, closing the door quietly behind him.

If Rachel were a horse? Amused at the thought, Cord sank down in the chair. Rachel was stubborn, high-spirited and unpredictable. Some trainers used whips on horses like that. His insides tightened at the thought. That kind of man trained a horse by breaking its spirit, taking away its heart.

If Rachel had been a horse, Cord knew he would have never tried to break that beautiful spirit by using a whip. He would have talked to her, touched her, made her trust him.

Not walked away.

He sat up so quickly his coffee sloshed over the sides of his cup onto his jeans, but he hardly noticed. He'd used his words and ultimatums like whips, trying to bend her to his will. *My way or no way.* He winced, remembering his words, then raked a hand through his hair and let out a long breath.

He'd wanted her to trust him, to let him take care of her, but he hadn't earned that trust by allowing her to make her own choices and decisions.

Sam was right, Cord thought, setting aside the coffee and tossing the whiskey into the trash. Solutions that create more problems aren't solutions.

Dragging a hand over his bristled chin, Cord stumbled out of the chair and headed for the bathroom. He frowned at the miserable sight of his own face as he leaned over the sink and stared in the mirror.

So what *was* the solution?

"It's time you came to your senses, Rachel."

Earl stood in front of her, his arms folded, his chin lifted in that arrogant, cocksure manner she'd always hated. She said nothing, just sat on the sofa, toying with a glass of ice water, and prepared herself for the litany that was sure to come. Seems that he'd been in touch with Mr. Raskin at the bank and somehow the news of Cord's leaving was in the process of spreading itself across town. It was all Earl had needed to hear to get him out to the ranch. He hadn't heard about the baby yet, though, she realized with a tremendous sense of relief. It had only been twenty-four hours since she'd heard herself, and it would take a little longer for Earl to learn that she was pregnant. She had no intention of telling him herself, though. As far as she was concerned, it was none of his business.

"You know," he went on, "you haven't been yourself since Michael's death. That's exactly why I've been so reluctant to relinquish control of your trust. I was afraid you might do something rash. Something you'd regret later."

She was already beginning to regret that she'd let him into the house, that she was even sitting here listening to his lecture. She wanted to tell him to go to hell, but she was just so tired, so damn weary of the fight.

"I have a buyer for the ranch, Rachel," he said. "Why don't you let me call him? You can move back to Dallas, see your friends again. There's a great condo available in my complex I can get you into. Think how easy your life will be."

Easy? Rachel thought as the pain coursed through her. Life without Cord would be the most difficult thing she'd ever had to face in her entire life. The only thing that kept her going right now was the baby.

She closed her eyes and nodded weakly. "Go ahead and call them." She took a sip of water, trying to wash away the foul taste those words left. What would it hurt to just listen to an offer? she thought bleakly.

The satisfaction of victory lighted Earl's face. He glanced at his gold watch. "I could probably get a-hold of the buyer now, but first, why don't we have a drink to celebrate?"

She'd sooner drink with a rattlesnake. "My stomach's a little queasy today. I'll pass."

Earl shrugged and moved to the bar. "You always did have a nervous stomach, honey. I never could figure out why you'd want to bring all that pressure on yourself and try to hang on to this run-down piece of dirt ranch."

Rachel had to bite the insides of her mouth so she wouldn't scream. Earl wouldn't understand what it meant to love something, or someone, so much you'd sacrifice anything to hold on to it or them. The baby was the only reason she was considering selling. She knew that with Cord gone the stress would be more than she could handle. She wouldn't jeopardize her baby's health, even to hold on to the Circle T.

Besides, she wiped away a drop of water on her glass, what did it matter anymore? Without Cord, the ranch no longer seemed like a home. It was quiet and lonely. Everywhere she turned, she thought of him. In her mind, she could see him working a horse in the corral, herding out a new load of cows, laughing with Sam and the other hands. She turned to him every night in bed, but he wasn't there, though his clothes hung in the closet and his razor still sat on the counter in the bathroom next to her brush.

Tears stung her eyes as she twisted the wedding band on her finger. Even if she removed every last trace of him, he'd still be in her heart. There'd be no way to erase his memory, or her love for him.

"Rachel."

She heard her name called and she glanced up. Earl sat down next to her. "I want you to know how sorry I am, about that man you married."

"Cord?" She lowered her brow. "What are you talking about?"

"I know it's hard for you, realizing that he left because he couldn't get his hands on your money."

Rachel was so stunned by Earl's words, she just stared at him. Then the anger began to build, slowly and steadily, like a pot coming to boil.

"Look, honey—" he took her hand in his "—everyone makes mistakes. Lord knows I have. Three wives and every one of them tried to take me to the cleaners. You don't have to be embarrassed. I'm here now. I'll help you."

"Get your hands off my wife."

Rachel and Earl both jumped at the sound of Cord's deathly quiet command. He stood in the doorway, his jean jacket under his arm and a package in his hand. His eyes were blazing with anger, his jaw set like stone.

Earl dropped Rachel's hand and stood. "Rumor had it you skipped town, Cantrell."

"Only people with manure for brains listen to rumors, Stephens." Cord tossed his jacket and the package on a chair by the sofa. He looked at Rachel and his expression softened. "You all right?"

Rachel simply nodded, dumbstruck at the sight of him standing there. Lord, but he looked good. Tired maybe, and his eyes were bloodshot, but good just the same.

"What are you doing here?" Cord turned back to Earl, his face once again a hard mask.

"Rachel's decided to sell the Circle T." He squared his shoulders.

"What!" Cord took a step toward her, then glanced back at Earl. "You sonofabitch. I should have known better than to turn my back on someone who crawls on their belly. It wasn't enough for you to swindle her out of her trust fund, now you're after the one thing that really means something to her."

"Watch what you say, Cantrell," Earl said angrily. "Or I'll have you in court for slander and fraud."

Rachel gasped as Cord's hand shot out and grabbed the front of Earl's starched shirt. "Let's do that. Let's go to court and see what the judge says when I tell him how you've been embezzling Rachel's money and dumping it into your own failing company."

Cord released him suddenly and Earl stumbled back, wiping at his jaw as if he'd been struck. His face had paled and a hint of fear touched the edges of his eyes.

Earl embezzling her money? Cord's words were like a slap. She jumped up, her heart beating so fast, she could feel it in her chest. "What are you talking about?"

Cord turned to her then. She could see him rein in his anger as he looked at her. "I'm sorry, Rachel. I didn't want to tell you like that."

She whirled and faced Earl. "Is it true? You've been milking my trust fund to support your own business?"

"It was temporary, Rachel." He straightened his shirt. "A loan. I was going to put the money back."

"All these months I've been breaking my back, worrying about how I was going to pay my bills and you've been using that money for your own selfish purposes?" She advanced on him, her fists clenched. "I always knew you were an arrogant, condescending swine, but I never dreamed you were a thief."

She spun away from him, afraid she might actually hit the man. "This is incredible. Michael, your own brother, leaves you my money to safeguard and you steal it."

"I didn't steal it," he protested. "I told you, I was going to put it back."

"And how were you going to do that?" Cord asked. "The Federal Trade Commission has slapped a lien on your company and seized your assets. The only thing they can't touch is what little is left in Rachel's trust, and this ranch. You must have been wringing your hands with joy when she told you she wanted to sell. A snake like you would have found some way to get your hands on that money, as well."

Panic registered on Earl's face. "I had some investments go sour. I would have recouped the money. I
still can. Rachel, just let me—"

"Get out of my house," she said stiffly. "You'll
hear from my lawyer and you can be sure you'll never
see another penny of my money."

"Rachel, honey—"

"Get out!" She thrust an arm toward the front
door. "And if you ever call me honey again, I swear
to you I'll put your lights out."

He stared at her for a moment, then cast an angry
glance at Cord before he squared his shoulders and
slammed out the front door.

Rachel stared after him, feeling empty inside, foolish. Her trust fund... How could she have been so
stupid? She turned slowly to Cord, her eyes narrowed. "How long have you known about this?"

"I suspected for a while, but I didn't know for sure
until yesterday. I had a broker friend of mine check
out Earl's company. When he told me the FTC had
seized the assets, I went to your bank and asked to see
records of any drafts made. There were several made
out to an obscure company. When I checked that
business out, I found out Earl was one of the key
stockholders. He was transferring the money out of
there and dumping it into his own account."

"You did all this, without asking me, without even
discussing it with me?"

Cord's shoulder twitched. "Calm down, Rachel. I
only did it to—"

"To save me?" She marched in front of him and
lifted her chin, meeting his intense gaze with her own.
"You leave for a week with no word, then come racing in here on a white horse to save the day and tell me

to calm down. I only have one thing to say to you, Cord Cantrell."

His jaw tightened. "What?"

"Thank you."

Cord heard the tone of Rachel's voice soften, and he saw the subtle lift at the corner of her lips, but he had steeled himself for a rebuke and it took a moment for her words to sink in. *Thank you.* So she wasn't angry at him. He allowed himself to breathe again. "You're welcome."

God, how he wanted to take her in his arms. She was wearing her hair in a French braid, like the first day they'd met; her eyes were large and provocative against her pale skin. She looked so beautiful, so feminine in the pink cotton dress she had on. There was something about her that was different, he noticed. If it were possible, something more appealing and seductive than he'd ever noticed before. He couldn't figure out what it was, but a starving man didn't question a gourmet meal when it was placed in front of him. He just devoured her with his eyes and his heart.

Patience, Cantrell. You promised yourself you'd move slowly.

He took a step back, only because there'd be no way to keep his hands off her if he didn't maintain some distance between them. But the smell of her, that light flowery scent, wafted around him and made his palms itch and his throat catch. "How are you, Rachel?"

How are you, Rachel? That's all he could say to her after a week? She watched him step away from her and she felt as if she were ripping into a thousand pieces. "I'm fine, Cord."

"I—I'm sorry about the trust fund. I've got the bank officials looking into recourse for you and—"

"You could have called me with this, Cord," she said, cutting him off. "Why did you come here?"

He shifted uncomfortably. "I, uh, saw Sam yesterday."

Her head snapped up at his words. Her heart began to pound. Did he know? Had Judy spoken to Sam and told him about the baby? The thought that Cord had come back because of the baby, and not for her, filled her with icy fingers of dread. Wrapping her arms around herself, she held his steady gaze. "Oh?"

Damn but she was making this difficult. Cord shoved his hands into the front pockets of his jeans. Why was she being so distant, so aloof? Maybe they hadn't parted on the best of terms, but he was still her husband, and whether she liked it or not, they had some things to discuss.

"Yes," he said with more annoyance than he intended. "He said some things that made me realize what a jerk I've been." He took a step closer, but still resisted reaching out to her, afraid she might pull away. "I can't leave you alone, Rachel. Especially not now."

He did know. Tears filled Rachel's eyes. Oh, God, how she'd hoped he'd come back because he loved her and needed her. She couldn't bear the thought of chaining a man like Cord to a marriage and child he didn't want. She felt the crushing, horrible weight of disappointment fill her. Her shoulders were trembling as she shook her head.

"No," she said, watching his expression harden as she spoke. "You don't have to worry about me being alone, Cord. I'll be fine. I still intend to sell the ranch, and that will take care of me and the baby for a long time while I try to decide what to do."

Cord had been so focused on her "no" that the rest of her words took a minute to absorb. "Baby?" he choked out. *"Baby?"*

Rachel's eyes widened and she stilled. "You—you didn't know?"

"Know?" Cord's voice rose. "I sure as hell didn't know. Just when were you going to get around to telling me?" He took an angry step closer. "Or was this one of your Miss Independent schemes and you decided you'd just handle this all by yourself?"

How dare he act as if he were the one who'd been wronged! She closed the gap between them and folded her arms indignantly. "I just found out yesterday, and besides, I'm not the one who stormed out of here a week ago, Cantrell. Perhaps if you'd bothered to leave a number, I might have called you."

"When?" he yelled. "On the kid's sixteenth birthday? You're trying to cut me out, Rachel, and I won't let you."

"You won't let me?" She poked a finger at his chest. "Is that why you came back? To intimidate me some more? To bully me and make me do things your way?"

"No."

"Then maybe it was just to collect your things and hit the road again." He shook his head and she continued angrily. "To protect me from Earl and save me from myself."

He clenched his jaw. "No."

She had to know. Whatever his reason, no matter what the truth was or how much it hurt, she had to know. "Then, why, Cord?" she shouted, her heart filled with fear and hope. "Why did you come back here?"

"Because I love you, dammit!"

It might not have been the most romantic, but it was the most wonderful, the most glorious admission she'd ever heard.

With a burst of laughter, Rachel threw her arms around Cord's neck. His body was taut with emotion, but gradually he relaxed. His arms came around her, pulling her tightly against him.

"I thought I'd go crazy without you this week." He buried his face in her neck and her hair.

"Me, too." Lord, but he felt good. She wound her arms tighter around his neck, never wanting to let go.

"A baby," he said softly. "Our baby."

"Cord." Rachel gasped. "I can't breathe."

"Oh, sorry." He loosened his grip on her, then set her away from him and ran a hand lovingly over her stomach. "When? How?"

She laughed. "The due date is March. And the how is pretty obvious."

He frowned. "I meant, we were always pretty careful."

"Not the first time. I thought that time was safe for me." She touched his cheek. "I'm so glad I was wrong."

He took her hand and brought it to his lips. "Rachel, speaking of being wrong, it was me who was wrong about forcing you to do things my way. My pride couldn't stand letting you be the boss and make all the decisions. I realize now how important that was to you, that you needed to make those decisions and find your own way in life. I'm sorry I tried to take that away from you."

"I was wrong, too, Cord." She gazed into his face and the love she saw there made her eyes prickle with moisture. "I was so consumed with the idea of never letting another man manipulate me or control me, I couldn't see the difference between being loved and protected. All you ever tried to do was help me and I was too stubborn to see that until now." Her fingers tingled where he kissed them. "I'm sorry I made things so difficult for you. I know now that compromise is not giving up control, but sharing it."

He smiled suddenly and pulled her to the chair, then lifted the package and handed it to her. "Open it."

Curious, Rachel took the bag and reached inside. What she pulled out made her heart swell with happiness.

A dinner bell.

Ignoring her tears, she wrapped her arms around Cord's waist. "I love you, Cord Cantrell."

His face lighted at her words. He kissed her gently then pulled away and lifted her chin with his index finger. "There is one thing, Rachel, one thing that I am going to have to insist on," he said sternly.

"What's that?"

He pressed his lips lightly to hers. "That you marry me."

She slid her arms around his neck. "I thought you'd never ask."

* * * * *

S SPRING FANCY

Three bachelors, footloose and fancy-free... until now!

Spring into romance with three fabulous fancies by three of Silhouette's hottest authors:

ANNETTE BROADRICK
LASS SMALL
KASEY MICHAELS

When spring fancy strikes, no man is immune!

Look for this exciting new short-story collection in March at your favorite retail outlet.

Only from

Silhouette®

where passion lives.

NORA ROBERTS

Love has a language all its own, and for centuries flowers have symbolized love's finest expression. Discover the language of flowers—and love—in this romantic collection of 48 favorite books by bestselling author Nora Roberts.

Two titles are available each month at your favorite retail outlet.

In March, look for:

The Art of Deception, Volume #27
Untamed, Volume #28

In April, look for:

Dual Image, Volume #29
Second Nature, Volume #30

Collect all 48 titles
and become fluent in
THE LANGUAGE of LOVE

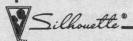
Silhouette®

MAN OF THE MONTH: 1993

They're tough, they're sexy...
and they know how to get the
job done....
Caution: They're

MEN AT WORK

Blue collar... white collar ... these men are working overtime to earn your love.

January:	Businessman Lyon Cantrell in Joan Hohl's LYON'S CUB
February:	Landscaper-turned-child-saver David Coronado in Raye Morgan's THE BACHELOR
March:	Woodworker Will Lang in Jackie Merritt's TENNESSEE WALTZ
April:	Contractor Jake Hatcher in Dixie Browning's HAZARDS OF THE HEART (her 50th Silhouette Book)
May:	Workaholic Cooper Maitland in Jennifer Greene's QUICKSAND
June:	Wheeler-dealer Tyler Tremaine in Barbara Boswell's TRIPLE TREAT

And that's just your first six months' pay! Let these men make a direct deposit into your heart. MEN AT WORK... only from Silhouette Desire!

SILHOUETTE® Desire®

HAWK'S WAY—where the Whitelaws of Texas run free till passion brands their hearts. A hot new series from Joan Johnston!

Look for the first of a long line of Texan adventures, beginning in April with THE RANCHER AND THE RUNAWAY BRIDE (D #779), as Tate Whitelaw battles her bossy brothers—and a sexy rancher.

Next, in May, Faron Whitelaw meets his match in THE COWBOY AND THE PRINCESS (D #785).

Finally, in June, Garth Whitelaw shows you just how hot the summer can get in THE WRANGLER AND THE RICH GIRL (D #791).

Join the Whitelaws as they saunter about HAWK'S WAY looking for their perfect mates . . . only from Silhouette Desire!